Walker's American History
series for young people

Straight Along
a
Crooked Road

Straight Along
a
Crooked Road

Marilyn Cram Donahue

Walker and Company
New York

Walker's American History Series for Young People
Frances Nankin, Series Editor

First published in the United States of America in 1985
by the Walker Publishing Company, Inc.

Published simultaneously in Canada by John Wiley & Sons
Canada, Limited, Rexdale, Ontario.

Printed in the United States of America

Library of Congress Cataloging in Publication Data

Donahue, Marilyn Cram.
  Straight along a crooked road.

  (Walker's American history series for young people)
  Summary: As her family travels from Vermont to settle
in California in the early 1850's, fourteen-year-old Luanna
learns to accept life for what it is, no matter where.
  [1. Overland journeys to the Pacific—Fiction.
2. Frontier and pioneer life—
Fiction. 3. West (U.S.)—Fiction] I. Title. II. Series.
PZ7.D71475St 1985   [Fic]   84–27118
ISBN 0-8027-6585-8

Book design by Teresa M. Carboni

10 9 8 7 6 5 4 3 2 1

To my mother,
who has traveled the road
and knows that every destination
is a new beginning.

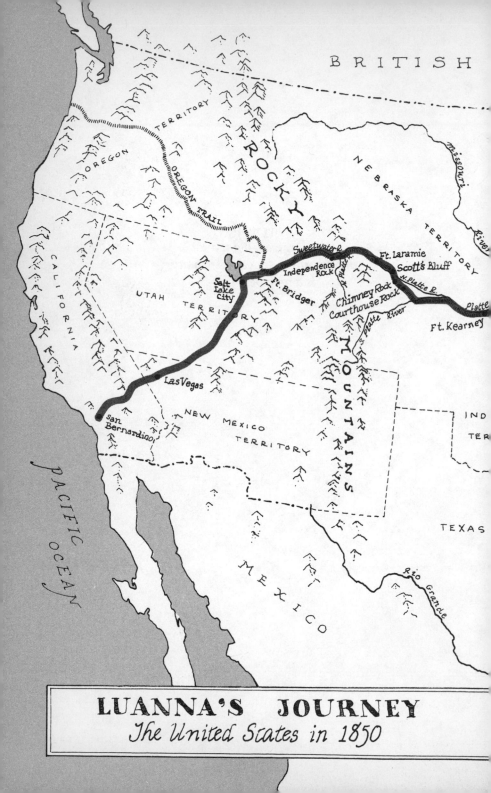

LUANNA'S JOURNEY
The United States in 1850

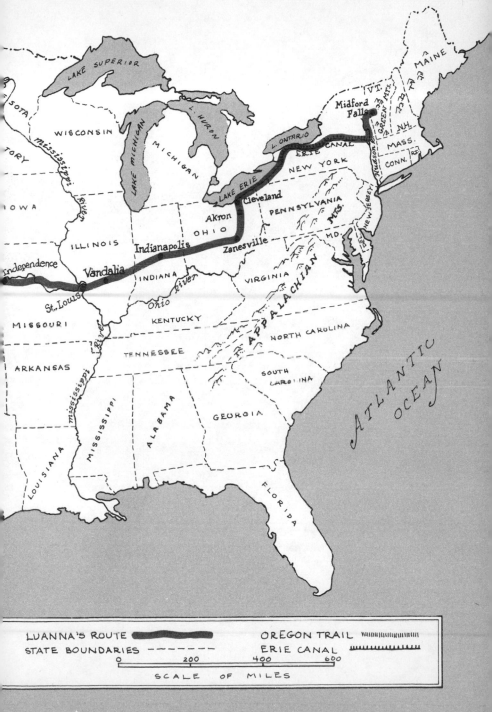

POSSESSIONS

LAKE SUPERIOR

WISCONSIN

MICHIGAN

LAKE MICHIGAN

L. HURON

MINNESOTA

TORY

IOWA

ILLINOIS

INDIANA

Independence

Vandalia

St. Louis

MISSOURI

Mississippi River

Ohio River

KENTUCKY

TENNESSEE

ARKANSAS

LOUISIANA

MISSISSIPPI

ALABAMA

GEORGIA

FLORIDA

Indianapolis

OHIO

Akron

Zanesville

Cleveland

LAKE ERIE

L. ONTARIO

ERIE CANAL

NEW YORK

PENNSYLVANIA

MD.

VIRGINIA

APPALACHIAN MTS.

NORTH CAROLINA

SOUTH CAROLINA

DEL.

NEW JERSEY

HUDSON R.

Midford Falls

VT.

GREEN MTS.

MAINE

N.H.

MASS.

CONN.

R.I.

ATLANTIC OCEAN

| LUANNA'S ROUTE | OREGON TRAIL |
| STATE BOUNDARIES | ERIE CANAL |

0   200   400   600

SCALE OF MILES

One

Luanna first heard the rumor on the Sunday before the Fourth of July in the year 1850. It was just a broken bit of conversation spoken at the edge of the churchyard.

"I'm talking about land, Daniel. Only a few dollars an acre, and in some places free for the living on it."

Luanna heard her father's voice. "We have land in Vermont, Jeremy. And schools for the children."

"And long, cold winters, and more people moving in every year. Four new families since spring. Before long there won't be any deer left to shoot. In California the weather's fine, and there's plenty of breathing room for everybody."

"I'll have to think on it. There's bound to be a good deal of risk . . ."

Jeremy made a snorting sound. "Risk is part of living! You know that. Think hard, man, and think fast. If you want to leave with me in the spring . . ."

They moved toward the front of the church and Luanna couldn't hear any more, but she had heard enough to know that Ian Douglas's father, Jeremy, had lost his mind.

Why would anyone want to go to California when he could live right here in Midford Falls, Vermont? She smiled to herself. When her father said he would think on it, he was just being polite. The Hamiltons would never leave Vermont. They never had.

Her father always said there were as many Hamilton names on the tombstones in the churchyard as there were live people sitting in the pews on Sunday mornings. Lots of times Luanna had walked with him among the stones and listened to stories about the great-uncles and -aunts and long-gone cousins. Her father's own Hamilton grandparents were buried on the crest of the hill. "We're rooted here," her father liked to say. "Just like that strong old oak that grows in the middle of the road. It's been there too long to be transplanted."

She hurried on around the side of the church to the water pump in back, where her friend Nancy Addison was waiting. Sunday morning services had finally ended, and Luanna felt the need to splash her face with cold water and clear her head. She pulled off her bonnet and bent over, working the pump a few seconds, then cupped her hands to catch the cold water.

"Long, wasn't it," commented Nancy. She had a large bandage over one eye and had only been able to splash one side of her face.

Luanna nodded. "Long and dull. Reverend Cochran preaches like he has to get through the whole Bible every Sunday. And we still have to sit through services again this afternoon." She looked at Nancy's bandaged eye. Pity, she thought, smiling at her friend. She was truly sorry when Nancy had an ailment. At the same time, she couldn't help feeling glad she wasn't sick herself. Poor Nancy always seemed to be catching or developing something.

"How does it feel?" she asked.

"Terrible. I hate having sties. This one feels as big as a boil. I wish I could give it away to someone."

"I don't blame you, but I don't want it. How about Belvidry Crawford? Here she comes now."

Belvidry approached them slowly. She looked hot and sweaty and her hair, freed from her bonnet, was wisping down into her eyes. She had that conceited look on her face that Luanna hated—the kind that said, "I'm sure everybody's watching me." She didn't say a word, just sidled up to the pump as if she owned it.

Nancy winked her good eye at Luanna and began to chant, "Sty, sty, go off my eye. Light on the first one passing by."

Belvidry didn't even finish splashing her face. She turned and walked straight up Cemetery Hill, zigzagging past the gravestones with large, marching steps that joggled the rest of her hair loose so that it fell down her back in long, dishwater-colored straggles.

"Look at her go," Luanna said. "Belvidry sure takes big steps, doesn't she?"

Nancy nodded. "Especially when she's mad. I guess I should have let her wash her face before I sent her packing. It's too hot to be mean today, and she does have a long walk home."

"Don't worry about Belvidry Crawford. She can cool off when she crosses the creek. Listen, Nance, have you heard Mr. Douglas talking about going to California?"

"He was out to our place last evening. Pa told him he must be crazy to think about leaving, especially since the railroad came through last year. What with the marble quarry and our merino sheep, Pa says 1850 looks good for Midford Falls. He says all the opportunity a body wants is right here under his nose."

"He's right," Luanna said. She had always liked Mr. Addison, and now she liked him more than ever.

"I don't know, Lu," Nancy replied. "You should have heard Mr. Douglas. He made California sound like the end of the rainbow. Sunshine all the year round. Land for everyone—good land that's not filled with rocks. The countryside is covered with trees and flowers, and there's plenty of good, fresh water. It sounded exciting, Lu. He made it seem like—like Paradise."

"He did, did he? Well, let me tell you something, Nancy Addison. If you're going to get all excited about finding Paradise, just open your eyes. You're standing right in the middle of it!" Luanna stretched her arms out wide. "Look at it, Nance. You can see the Green Mountains over to the east, and buttercups are blooming in Long Meadow. The sugar maples are in full leaf on the hill. There are wild strawberries down on the banks of Otter Creek and cat-tails growing in the marsh. You can sip honeysuckle in the summer and go barefoot in the river. You can slide on winter ice and eat maple-sugar-on-snow. This is Vermont! I love it so much I'm never going to leave it."

"That's all right with me." Nancy was laughing. "But you'd better stop throwing your arms around like that. Last time you ripped your seams clear to the waist."

Luanna grinned and lowered her arms. "Oh, Nance, that's just like you. What would I do if you weren't around to bring me back to earth?"

"Rip a lot of seams, I suppose. All the same, Lu, you have to admit there's something exciting about the idea of going west. Just think of it! New things to see every day —different things—some of them strange and some of them wonderful."

"But it's dangerous, Nance. Don't forget that. And there are lots of hardships. Bumping along all day in a wagon for weeks at a time is not what I call fun."

Nancy agreed. "It would take a lot of courage to go," she said. "Remember last year in school when Miss Wilson said that pioneers are special people? Do you think we could be pioneers, Lu? I wonder what it would be like. I wonder if we could do it if we had to."

"Don't bother your head wondering," Luanna told her. "I for one don't intend to find out."

She thought that ended the matter, but that night at the supper table she found out that Jeremy Douglas had been stirring up the whole town with his foolishness. "He's been going house to house," her father said, "trying to get folks interested."

Luanna's mother gave a little laugh. "Jeremy's a fine man and a good neighbor, but he does get overexcited. I don't imagine folks are paying him any mind."

Her father pushed his plate away and leaned way back in his chair, making it balance on its two back legs. Luanna thought he took a good while to answer. "Jeremy does have a point, Rebecca. There's opportunity in the West."

"I'll say there is!" exclaimed Ben. Luanna had four brothers, and they did a lot of talking, but Benjamin, who was sixteen and the oldest, could be counted on to make the most noise.

"They say the animals are running through the woods so thick a body trips on them," he announced. "The water's so sweet you'd think it was sugared. And the gold is lying on the ground, ready to be picked up and weighed."

Luanna stared at him. Ben usually had better sense than to believe stories like that. But he wasn't the only one who was all stirred up. The rest of them talked so loud and fast that five-year-old Emmie got down out of her chair and went to sit on her mother's lap. When Nathaniel started in about the Indians and what he would do if they tried to scalp him, Emmie began to cry.

All the time, Eli was trying hard to be heard, but nobody was listening. Almost fifteen, he was as tall as his father, but slender as a reed. Luanna's mother always said that Eli was the only one who could sit still in church. He seldom had much to say, but when he did, it was usually worth hearing. "I believe . . . I think we should . . ." Luanna heard those words, and then a whole sentence. "I would like to see the Pacific Ocean," Eli said.

Everyone was silent a moment, looking at him. His words had somehow reminded them that California was a whole continent away. Then Nathaniel, who was never quiet for long, decided to imitate an Indian war cry. He looked straight at Emmie and began tapping his fingers against his mouth. "Ahh-wah-wah-wah," he chanted, until their mother threatened to send him away from the table.

Luanna wondered why her father never said a word. He didn't eat much for supper, either. Just listened to all the talking and glanced every now and then at her mother. Luanna kept quiet too. She knew that even if she told her brothers how silly they sounded, they would never hear her.

For the next three days the whole town was getting ready for their Fourth of July celebration, and California seemed to be a forgotten subject. The church bell woke Luanna up on the Fourth when it began ringing for a whole hour at sunrise. By midmorning people were arriving from smaller neighboring towns to join in the festivities and listen to the hourly boom of the cannon on the green.

At eleven o'clock the parade began. The war veterans led the way, followed by horse-drawn carts decorated with red, white, and blue ribbons. Jeremy Douglas walked along playing his bagpipes and wearing the kilt that he put on for special occasions. At the end came a group of younger school children, waving at their parents and anyone else who would wave back. They all started north of town by the schoolhouse and marched along Main Street in front of the church, once around the green, and out of town in the other direction, ending up in the open field next to the blacksmith's shop.

Luanna met Nancy in front of Midford House, the town inn, and they climbed the front steps and sat on the porch railing so they could see. Some of the veterans played fifes and drums, and the music made chills go up Luanna's spine, even in the hot July weather. There was no place like this, she thought. No place in the world like Midford Falls, Vermont.

After the parade, the Declaration of Independence was read by the town clerk, and there were speeches by visiting preachers. Finally came recitations and songs performed by the pupils from the school. "Aren't you glad we don't have to do that this year?" Luanna whispered.

Nancy nodded, then reached out and gave Luanna a sharp poke in the ribs. "Look who's going to entertain us."

Belvidry Crawford was climbing the steps of the bandstand. When she reached the top, she turned and faced the audience on the green. "She's going to be reciting for years to come," Luanna said. "She's older than we are and still in the fifth grade."

"Oh, my," whispered Nancy. "Look at the poor thing." The hem of Belvidry's skirt sagged a little on one side, and the cuffs of her long sleeves hit her halfway up the arms. Belvidry took a deep breath and began to recite. She was doing fine until a thickening mass of white began to gather at the bottom of her skirt. She stopped in the middle of her recitation, glanced down, then went right on, talking faster and faster.

"It's her drawers," Nancy hissed. "Belvidry's losing her drawers."

She isn't losing them. She's lost them, Luanna thought. They fell right down to the wooden floorboards of the bandstand and hung around her ankles.

"Oh, Lu, what's she going to do?" Nancy had both hands over her face, trying not to laugh. "Tell me what happens. I can't look."

Luanna couldn't stop looking. She watched Belvidry's face turn red. It seemed as red as the powdered ochre that Mr. Hamilton mixed with buttermilk and used for paint. But she never stopped reciting until she was finished. Then she made a little bow, stooped over and stepped out of her drawers, put them over one arm, and climbed down off the platform. A few people clapped, but there were lots of snickers, too. Luanna thought if that had happened to her, she would have dropped dead on the grass. But Belvidry walked across the green, crossed the road, and disappeared among the gravestones behind the church on Cemetery Hill.

"Maybe we should go find her," Nancy said.

"I don't think she'd appreciate that. Not after you offered her your sty like you did."

Nancy giggled. "Then let's go watch the potato races."

Luanna thought that the Fourth of July was the best celebration of the year. Nobody told you to mind your manners, or even seemed to care where you went. Music from the bandstand drifted across the green, floating above their heads, just out of reach. The mouth-watering smells of ham and mutton and blueberry slump filled the air. Big pots of beans, loaves of dark bread, and piles of corn on the cob were washed down with cool glasses of lemonade. And for a summer treat, there was ice cream, frozen by old Mr. Burke, who kept an ice house down by the river. Luanna knew that he beat up the ingredients, put them in his old pot freezer, and shook it up and down in a pan of ice and salt. She had wandered by there one day, and he had let her help. It was awfully hard on your arms to make ice cream, Luanna decided. But it did taste good in July!

Exhibitions were placed on long tables. There were handicrafts, crocheted lace, pickles, preserves, and straw bonnets. Prizes were given in cash, or sometimes silver spoons. To top everything off, there was a greased pig to catch. All Luanna's brothers had a try, but it was eleven-year-old Tink who captured the pig. He circled it slowly, which was the way Tink always went after a problem. Then he threw himself at it so suddenly that the animal didn't know which way to run.

All day long, even when she was in the middle of having a good time, Luanna kept thinking about Belvidry. She didn't like her, but she felt sorry for her just the same.

"Belvidry has a lot of pluck," she told Nancy. "I would have died if my drawers had come off."

Nancy nodded. "My pa says the Crawfords have plenty of sass. He says maybe it will stand them in good stead on the trip."

"What trip? What are you talking about?"

"Didn't I tell you? The whole Crawford family is going to California."

Luanna didn't say a word. But she was remembering how Belvidry's face had turned so red, and she was thinking of all the people who had snickered. She had felt like snickering herself, and Nancy had giggled right out loud. It might be the best thing if Belvidry left town. Luanna was sure of it. It was a good thing Belvidry Crawford was going to California.

Two

People were saying they had never seen such a hot summer. Otter Creek was running so low that the sandy bottom had surfaced in spots. The meadow grass was parched, and when the stage came in three times a week and stopped in front of Midford House, it brought with it a rolling cloud of dust that settled over the front porch and stayed there. Mr. Thompson, who ran the general store, said these were "dog days," and that they meant a long, cold winter.

"Nobody talks about anything else," Luanna complained. "It's nothing but the weather from sunup to sunset."

"Well, it *is* hot," her mother said, "and I'd rather hear weather talk than California talk. *That* is getting just plain tiresome." She pushed damp hair back from her forehead. "I'm going to peel some potatoes."

She would have to peel a whole basket of them, Luanna thought, to fill this family up. And it would be worse in a few days. Aunt Prue and Uncle Fisk Hamilton always came for a visit at the end of August, bringing Great-aunt

Clara with them. They would stay for two terrible weeks. When they left, Great-aunt Clara would remain. It had been that way for as long as Luanna could remember. Aunt Clara would live with them for half the year and then Mr. Hamilton would take her back up the road to Vergennes to live the other half with Uncle Fisk, his brother.

Luanna began to set the table for the midday meal. Sweat was rolling down her back between her shoulder blades, and she felt damp and sticky all over. Still and all, she didn't mind the heat as much as the waiting.

Last month she and Nancy had passed the tests that would admit them to the Essex Female Academy in the fall. The academy was in the big building up the hill north of town, set way back from the road in its own meadow. Midford Falls College was a little distance beyond, but you had to be born a boy if you wanted to go there.

Ben could have gone, but he wasn't interested. Eli couldn't make up his mind. Mr. Hamilton said if that's the way he felt, he wasn't going to put any money out on him. So Luanna was the first of the Hamiltons to go beyond the eighth grade, and she knew she wouldn't be going at all if Miss Wilson hadn't come and talked her father into it. He wasn't sure it was a good idea, he said. Girls didn't need that much schooling. Look at his wife, Rebecca. She hadn't gone past the eighth grade.

His wife had stared at him hard, her eyes narrowed and her mouth tight. She didn't say a word, but Miss Wilson jumped right in with both feet. "Your wife is an exceptional woman, Mr. Hamilton. I'm sure she has educated herself far beyond that level." Luanna saw her mother's mouth begin to twitch.

Miss Wilson knew when she had the advantage. "You must try to understand," she went on, "that Luanna is an excellent student. You know she got top honors from the grammar school in June. With a little more education she can make her mark in the world—teaching, perhaps. Or she might even become a writer."

Mr. Hamilton didn't think much of the writer part. But teaching was an honorable profession. The upshot was that Luanna would enter the academy in the fall. Sometimes she didn't know if she could wait until the next three weeks were over. It was going to seem a lot longer than that with Aunt Prue there.

Luanna wiped the sweat off her face. In a little while her father would close up the cooperage and ride in from town, and all her brothers who were old enough to work in the fields would burst into the house—sweaty, noisy, and hungry. Her father didn't spend much time in the fields except at planting and harvesting time. He had plenty of sons, he said, to do the farming for him.

Eli had complained about that once. "He ought to take his turn sweating," he had said. Luanna had never seen her mother so angry. "Your pa knows more about sweat than any ten men," she snapped. "He was farming before you ever saw a plow, and he'd rather be farming now. But he's making barrels because it's profitable, and it takes profit to keep this family going."

Luanna knew that Eli didn't like working in the fields any better after that, but he did keep his mouth shut. She didn't feel a bit sorry for him. He could have avoided the fields altogether if he had decided to go on to school. "What's the matter with you?" she had asked him. "It didn't take me five minutes to make up my mind."

"Pa's coming! Pa's coming!" cried Nathaniel. He appeared out of nowhere the way he always did, made a quick inspection to see what was cooking, and ran out the back door, slamming it behind him.

"Your pa's early," her mother said, wiping her hands on her apron and smoothing her hair. Luanna thought her mother's hair was beautiful. Dark and shiny and brushed up and away from her face, she caught it at the sides with two tortoise shell combs and wound it into a thick figure eight in back. People said Luanna had her mother's good looks. She hoped they were right.

She knew she was tall for her age, and slender, and her friend Amy Douglas said that she had nice eyes. "Bluish gray, like the sky at twilight," Amy told her. "And your lashes are so long and dark." Amy noticed other people's lashes because hers were so blonde they were almost invisible.

Mr. Hamilton came into the house with a smile on his face. He went straight to his wife and put his arms around her. "I'm a little early, Rebecca," he said.

"I can see that, Daniel." Luanna's mother pulled back and looked at him long and hard. "You've got something on your mind," she said.

Luanna suddenly felt uncomfortable, as if she were eavesdropping, even though nobody was saying a word. They just stood there and looked at each other a long time. Finally Mrs. Hamilton gave a long sigh and leaned her head on her husband's chest.

"You've decided," she said.

"Yes, Rebecca."

"We're going then?"

"Yes. Come spring."

Mrs. Hamilton didn't move for a minute. She leaned there against him, and he held her that way, his cheek resting against her soft hair. Then, she raised her head and smiled. "Dinner's ready," was all she said.

Dinner's ready. As if nothing in the world had changed. *Dinner's ready.* As if life were going on as usual. Luanna tried to sort through what she'd heard. She ran it through her mind again, wiping it away, the way she used to wipe her slate clean. But the words reappeared. *We're going, then? . . . Yes. Come spring.* No one had said California, but Luanna heard it just the same. Where else did people head for in the spring? She suddenly felt dizzy, reached for a chair, and sat down hard.

Nancy had told her once that drowning people had their whole lives flash right before their eyes. Luanna hadn't believed it. But she felt as if she were drowning now, and everything in the kitchen was turning to a dull, smoky gray, while the things she loved about Midford Falls seemed to stand out sharp and clear. She thought in quick succession of the covered bridge on the quarry road, the waterfall at the mill pond, the lacy ferns at the edge of the cattail marsh, the old schoolhouse, the feel of river water on her bare feet, the taste of cold cider. And she thought of Nancy, and the academy, and the soft sounds of the first snow.

The door flew open, and Ben burst into the room. Luanna blinked hard to bring him into focus. His face was red from the heat, but it was clean and his hair was combed. Eli and Tink followed, and they looked the same as Ben.

"Is everybody here?" Mr. Hamilton asked. He looked around the room, counting heads, then went to the back door and rattled the cow bell that hung from a piece of rope. Nathaniel appeared, and Emmie was with him. "When we're all at the table, I'll tell you some news," Mr. Hamilton said. "What are you doing sitting there, Lu? Get up and help your mother put dinner on the table."

Luanna got up and began carrying platters of cold sliced ham and bowls of boiled vegetables to the table. Loaves of fresh bread were still warm from the oven. Her mother went into the stone pantry and brought out two pitchers of cool milk with froth on top. On the sideboard were three blackberry pies.

Dinner's ready. Just as if the end of the world wasn't

about to come. Luanna tried not to look at all that food. It made her feel sick.

Mr. Hamilton cleared his throat. "Is everybody listening?" The room got quiet. Luanna looked out the east window to where the hill behind the house was covered with sugar maples. "Come spring," he said, "we're going to make a change. I've always wanted the best for my family, and up till now I thought the best was right here in Midford Falls. It is good here, but it's not right to close your eyes to opportunity. The country is changing, and I think California is the place to be."

For a few seconds no one said a word. Then Ben asked, "Does that mean we're really going?"

"It does." Mr. Hamilton helped himself to some ham and cut a thick slice of bread. "Now eat your dinner," he said, as if nothing had changed at all.

The noise started like the hum of a single bee and grew until it was a swarm. Luanna's brothers all seemed to be talking at once—wondering in loud, excited voices what they should take, how long a trip it would be, who in Midford Falls might be going with them. Then, little by little, the words began to drop away, leaving small silences that grew longer and longer until a heavy quiet settled over the big table.

Luanna noticed that Eli was spreading his food around on his plate, but not putting any of it into his mouth. Ben was looking at his father, and Tink's smile was turning lopsided. Nathaniel was quiet for once—he sat still and watched the others. Emmie stopped eating and began to hiccup. She put both hands over her mouth, but she didn't stop.

"Oh, Emmie, take a drink of water!" exclaimed her mother. Emmie did, and then she hiccuped again. It was the only noise in the room—Emmie's hiccuping.

What had happened to her brothers? Luanna wondered.

All they'd talked about for weeks was going to California. And now that they were going, nobody had a thing to say. Her mother met her eyes across the table and seemed to read her thoughts. "Talking is different from doing," she said softly. Then she got up quickly and took Emmie out of the room.

Luanna looked across the table at her father. Would he understand how she felt if she told him? She took a shaky breath. "I don't want to go," she said.

Surprisingly, he smiled. "Of course you don't, Lu. Why, I'll bet you feel like the world's coming to an end, don't you?" He pushed back his plate and got up. "Don't you remember, Lu, a few years back when old Mr. Miller felt the same way? Why, he believed it so sincerely he went all over the countryside telling folks when it was going to happen. When the big day came, he climbed up on his barn so he could fly to heaven at midnight."

Luanna remembered, and so did her brothers. Midford Falls had never had anything like that happen before or since. "Well," Mr. Hamilton continued, "he fell down and broke a leg and bashed himself up real good. The world didn't end for him, and it won't for you either. You wait and see. In a few days, you'll be happy about this."

Luanna didn't answer. No matter what he said about the world, she knew that her life in Midford Falls was over.

Three

That very afternoon she had to go tell Miss Wilson her school plans had changed. It was only fitting, her mother told her, when Miss Wilson had gone to so much trouble for her. Luanna found the teacher in the schoolhouse, dusting and cleaning the one big room, getting ready for opening day.

"Luanna—what a nice surprise! Are you excited about starting at the academy?"

"I—I was, but not anymore. Oh, Miss Wilson, Pa says we're going to California in the spring."

Miss Wilson's smile faded and disappeared. "Are you sure? I mean, is it definite?"

Luanna nodded. "I don't want to go. Pa says it's not the end of the world, but it is for me. Oh, Miss Wilson, I'd do anything to stay here in Midford Falls."

Miss Wilson put her arm around Luanna's shoulders. "What a waste," she murmured. "What a terrible waste."

It was even worse when Luanna told Nancy, who started to cry and wouldn't stop. "What will I do without you?" she sobbed. "Nothing will ever be the same again."

Nobody had to tell Luanna that—or that it was a wilderness out West—or that she would see Belvidry Crawford every single day. But Nancy did. And then she said a very strange thing. "I—I wish I was going with you, Lu."

There was no figuring people out, Luanna decided. They all seemed to want what they couldn't get. She walked along the dusty path that wound through a field of red clover and was the shortest route home from the Addison farm. She stopped along the way to pick a dandelion puff and blow the little seeds to kingdom come. But she didn't make a wish. There didn't seem to be any use.

She was almost home when she heard the voice. There was no mistaking the sound of Aunt Prue. She sounded for all the world like a crow. Luanna rounded the last curve where the path went through a stand of tamarack trees and ended at the side of the vegetable garden near the back door.

"Well, there's Luanny," Aunt Prue shrieked. "Pick up your feet, girl, and you won't raise so much dust when you walk."

Luanna sighed. They had come early again. Aunt Prue always claimed it gave them a few extra days to visit, but Luanna knew it was because she liked to come up on people unawares. Luanna had seen her slip into the parlor and run her finger over the back of a chair. She was always looking for somebody else's dust, and never happy unless she found some.

The next two weeks were long ones. When Aunt Prue found out about California, she pointed her finger right under Mrs. Hamilton's nose. "If my Fisk started talking foolish, I'd put a stop to it right off."

"That's the difference between you and me, Prue. I don't think Daniel talks foolish."

That stopped Aunt Prue for a minute, but only until she realized that she was going to have Great-aunt Clara full time. "I don't know how I'll manage," she complained. "After all, Rebecca, my house isn't near as roomy as yours." She stopped short. "But you won't be needing this big house any longer, will you?" Luanna thought her eyes began to gleam right then.

She must have gone to work on Uncle Fisk that very day. The first thing anybody knew, he was offering to sell out at Vergennes and buy Mr. Hamilton's cooperage as well as the house and farm. They would move down here in the spring and take right over.

"Isn't it lucky?" Aunt Prue crowed. "Things are working out dandy for everyone."

Not everyone, Luanna thought. And she wasn't the only one who felt that way. Late one night, after all the company had left, she heard voices in the parlor and crept to the stairs to listen. She knew she was eavesdropping, but the old rules didn't seem to count for much these days.

"Prue dresses fancy and thinks big," her mother was saying, "but she's common, Daniel. I won't have that woman living in my house."

"Rebecca." His voice was gentle. "It won't be your house when she's living in it."

Luanna felt as if someone had pulled a rug out from under her and sent her spinning. Even when she knew Aunt Prue would be living here after they were gone, she had never thought of this as Aunt Prue's house. The voices went on, but Luanna couldn't stand to hear another word.

She crept to her bed and pulled the covers over her ears. *Won't be your house . . . won't be your house . . .* In a few months, this wouldn't be Luanna's house either. Then where would home be? Not one of those wagons her father was building. She squeezed her eyes shut. Never, never would she call a wagon home!

Just before school started in September, Miss Wilson

came to call. Mrs. Hamilton took her into the parlor, and Luanna's father went in after them, closing the door behind him. Luanna didn't even hesitate. She put her ear close to the crack the way she had seen Ben do, and listened.

"If you would let her stay with me for a year or two—" Miss Wilson was saying.

Mr. Hamilton didn't even let her finish. He cleared his throat the way he always did when he was about to say something final. "I know you mean well, Miss Wilson, but Luanna is my daughter. I don't intend leaving her behind."

"Then won't you at least let her start school next week and continue her studies until spring?"

"The academy is expensive. I'm afraid we're going to need all the cash we can save."

"Is that your final word, Mr. Hamilton?"

"It is."

"Then I have one last request. Will you allow me to gather together some lessons for Luanna? A few things she can read and study along the way—some books, perhaps, that will—"

"Books are expensive, Miss Wilson. Luanna can't possibly accept such a—"

"Of course she can." It was her mother's voice. "We're grateful to you, Miss Wilson, for your thoughtfulness. Luanna will be, too."

Luanna's mother did that sometimes—stepped in just in time when her father was about to say no. But she never did it unless it really mattered. And when she did, Mr. Hamilton let her have her say.

So Miss Wilson brought the books, and Luanna packed them carefully away. There were pens, too, and two bottles of ink and a thick package of paper, just like they used over at the academy. Luanna held the paper, feeling it with her fingers, then packed it away too, remembering that school had started this year without her.

One afternoon the stage brought the news that California had become a state. It had happened on September 9, 1850, but when word came to Midford Falls the following month, you would have thought it was another Fourth of July, the way Luanna's brothers carried on, hopping up and down and cheering as if they'd won a war. "At least you won't be leaving the country, Lu," Nancy told her. Sometimes Luanna thought Nancy was missing the whole point.

The apples ripened and it was cider time. Mr. Hamilton climbed down the back side of Cemetery Hill and crossed over to the far side of the cattail marsh where Josiah Adams kept a cider still. He brought home several barrels of cider brandy. "For medicinal purposes on the road," he said. It was the first time Luanna could remember that her mother had allowed cider brandy in the house.

When Thanksgiving came, Luanna couldn't see that there was much to be thankful for. Especially when Aunt Prue and Uncle Fisk made the trip from Vergennes to spend a week with them.

"Isn't this nice?" Aunt Prue exclaimed. "It gives me a chance to look around and see what I want to change. Rebecca, dear, you know you can't take all this with you. Let's go through the house together and decide what you want to leave."

"Humph!" said Aunt Clara. "Don't you have any manners at all, Prue?"

Luanna guessed her aunt didn't, and she was glad when Uncle Fisk finally took her home. Christmas was coming, and she didn't think she could stand to have Aunt Prue around for that. To her surprise, she found that Aunt Clara agreed with her.

"That woman," she snorted, "will be the death of me! I'd

almost rather go to California than spend another day in her house." Luanna looked at her in surprise. "Almost," Aunt Clara snapped.

The winter brought heavy snowfalls, and the weather was icy cold. "The sun shines all the year round in California," Nathaniel told her. Well, there was some merit to that, she thought, as she tried to thaw her frozen fingers by the fire. But not a lot.

She thought of the skating pond, the feel of stepping in fresh soft snow clear up to her knees, the crunch of it beneath her feet, the slipping and sliding down the hill above Long Meadow. She looked out the window at the lacy patterns of ice on the trees, and she thought she had never seen anything so beautiful.

But when she went to the mill pond to watch the men cut ice to store for the summer, she realized that her father was cutting it for Uncle Fisk and Aunt Prue. She stood there only a few minutes, then turned and walked away. There were parts of Midford Falls that weren't hers anymore. For the first time, she began to feel as if she didn't belong.

In January, Luanna turned fourteen. "It's my last birthday in Midford Falls," she told Nancy. "I just wish I could die right now so you could bury me here."

"Please don't talk like that, Lu. Look, I brought you a present." Nancy was holding a package wrapped in white paper. "Go on, open it."

It was a metal box with a hinged lid. It looked like a miniature trunk, and was about as large as the family Bible that lay on the table by the front window. Luanna lifted the latch and opened it. Inside were two crimson leaves that had been pressed flat, a small paperweight of polished red marble, and a rolled-up piece of paper tied with a bit of red ribbon saved from the Fourth of July.

"It's a memory box," Nancy told her. "The autumn leaves and red marble are to remind you of Midford Falls.

You can add whatever you like, but you have to promise not to open the letter until you reach Illinois."

They were stopping in Illinois to spend the next winter—Jeremy Douglas and Luanna's father and even Tyler Crawford had agreed that it was far enough for starters. Then they would push on to Independence, Missouri, early in the spring and join a wagon train moving west. That way they wouldn't be greenhorns when they began the hardest part of the trip.

"We need some experience on the road," Mr. Hamilton explained. "We'll take it slow," he promised. "From Midford Falls to Illinois will seem like a vacation. Think of it, Rebecca, you won't have any housework to do."

Luanna's mother gave him a long look, but she didn't say a word. After that, whenever she dusted the furniture Luanna saw her run her fingers over each piece, slowly, lovingly. And Luanna knew that most of it was going to be left behind for Aunt Prue.

February came and went, and Aunt Clara stayed on. "There's plenty I can help with here," she said, "and I'll be living with Prue soon enough."

Luanna hated the way Aunt Clara bustled around all day, putting her nose where it didn't belong. Even in the evenings she sat there smoking her clay pipe and telling them what they should do.

Sugaring began the first week of March, and the air was sweet with the smell of maple sap cooking until the syrup thickened. Mrs. Hamilton boiled most of it down and poured it into wooden tubs to harden into sugar that they would take with them on the trip. But there was plenty of syrup left over to pour in swirling streams over clean white snow. Luanna and Nancy wound the sticky candy on flat, wooden spoons and ate it with sour pickles and fresh wheat doughnuts. Luanna wondered if she would ever taste anything that good again.

It seemed to her that they spent the whole long winter

getting ready to leave. They made more soap than Luanna had ever seen. Tallow candles were dipped and packed away. When the cobbler came through town on his circuit, everybody got shoes—sturdy ones that would stand some walking. Luanna hated them because the soles were pegged with wooden pegs and both feet were alike, but her father said they would be easy to mend on the trail.

There were clothes to be made—out of common homespun, which Luanna thought was ugly compared with the silks they could order from Boston. Mrs. Hamilton dyed her yarn with butternut bark instead of indigo, which was expensive. Pokeberry would have made a beautiful shade of vermilion, but Aunt Clara said butternut-dyed homespun was more practical for where they were going.

Spring seemed to arrive suddenly, and the wild passenger pigeons flew over Midford Falls like great clouds with beating wings. Luanna walked through the fields looking for the first red-winged blackbird, hunting for the first golden crocuses poking up out of thin patches of melting snow. She paid a last visit to the schoolhouse and the mill pond, and she walked around the green, passing her father's cooperage and the general store. One morning she stood on the old covered bridge listening to the sound of Otter Creek as it swelled and ran over its banks. In the afternoon, she and Nancy hiked past the sawmill and climbed the winding trail to the top of Snake Mountain. They could see the long sweep of Lake Champlain on the west with the Adirondacks beyond, and on the east were the Green Mountains.

"What's the matter with everybody, talking about room to see?" she asked Nancy. "We can see in Vermont, for pity's sake!"

Nancy sighed. "Oh, Lu, you're going to see so much more than this. I do wish I could go with you!"

"Don't say that!" Luanna told her. "You've got to stay here. If you were to leave, who would I come home to?"

Nancy stared at her. "Come home to?"

"Yes, I've made up my mind. Somehow I'm going to come back, even if I have to come all the way from California by myself. I can live with you, can't I?"

"Of course you can, Lu, but—"

"Don't you go *anywhere*, Nance. You're my only hope. Promise me right now that you'll be here when I come home."

"But—but what if it takes years and years?"

Luanna made an impatient face. "Don't worry, it won't. And when I come back, I'm going to stay here forever."

As the weather warmed, the packing began. Trunks were filled, and decisions were made. Someone had to choose which books, and dishes, and mementoes, and furniture to leave behind. "I can't leave everything," Mrs. Hamilton moaned. "I have to take some part of civilization with me."

"I wish you'd leave me," Luanna muttered. She expected to be scolded and was surprised when her mother stopped what she was doing and put both arms around her and held her tight.

The two wagons were finished and canvas hoods were stretched high over bent hickory bows to make a tall, protective covering. They were sturdy-looking wagons with heavy sideboards, and the wheels were rimmed with iron. Luanna hated the sight of them and kept as far away from them as she could. "They make me feel awful," she confided to Nancy. "When I look at them, I can't pretend we're not going anymore."

Unfortunately, Aunt Clara heard her. "You're a very stubborn girl," she said. "It's a trait that may stand you in good stead on the trip. But you must learn that there are times when you have to give over and accept a situation you can't change."

Luanna glared at her and didn't answer, so Aunt Clara marched her out to the side yard and made her take a good long look at the wagons. "You'd better get acquainted," she said. "You're going to be seeing a lot of each other." Then she walked Luanna around each one, showing her where the butter churn would hang, where the water barrels were already strapped on, and where Mr. Hamilton's plow would be attached at the side of one wagon. "Everything that can't hang on the outside goes in here." Aunt Clara lifted a canvas flap and pointed to the wagon boxes. "All your furniture, clothes, and food. See where your ma sewed big pockets and such on the inside of the canvas so you can store more?"

Luanna sniffed. "There isn't enough room for all that and us, too. Where are we going to sit?"

Aunt Clara stared at her. "You have two good legs, don't you? You can right well walk!"

Luanna clamped her mouth shut tight. There wasn't any use telling Aunt Clara she was crazy. They'd be rid of her soon enough. It was about the only good thing Luanna could see about going to California. They would be leaving Aunt Clara behind, and Aunt Prue could deal with her sharp tongue forever and ever.

But that night at dinner, Aunt Clara made an announcement. "If you'll have me," she said, "I'm coming with you. This house won't be the same without all of you in it. I know I'm an old woman, but I'm strong, and I won't hold anybody back. Anyway, I'll likely live longer on the trail than sitting here listening to Prue."

Luanna's father smiled. "We'll be happy to have you," he said. "Won't we, everybody?"

Luanna was the only one who didn't say a word. She didn't trust herself to open her mouth.

At last the day came in early May when the roads were passable and the grass in the fields was green enough to feed the stock. "We'll load the wagons today," said Mr. Hamilton, "and start out first thing tomorrow morning."

Their extra eggs were packed in cornmeal, and thick slabs of bacon were layered in a barrel of bran. Heavy trunks and pieces of furniture went in the wagons first, and everything else had to fit around and on top of those. Food supplies and Mrs. Hamilton's Dutch oven had to be placed where they could be easily unpacked. At the last moment Luanna's mother decided to pack the cherrywood clock that sat on the mantel and the tea set with the moss rose design. Luanna knew it was because she couldn't bear the thought of Aunt Prue telling time by the one or drinking tea out of the other.

A seat was fixed for Aunt Clara in the back of one wagon. Luanna noticed with satisfaction that she would be packed in tight between the bacon and the beans. Maybe when she saw how she was going to have to travel, she'd change her mind and stay.

But she didn't. The next morning she climbed in all by herself, slapping Eli's hand when he tried to help her. Mrs. Hamilton swept out the parlor for the last time and closed the front door. She took one long look at the house, then turned away. Mr. Hamilton helped her onto the wagon seat, then lifted Emmie up to sit beside her. He had hitched three yoke of oxen to each wagon. Two cages of cackling chickens hung beneath each wagon bed. Tink and Nathaniel were herding a dozen bleating sheep and trying to keep an eye on Molly and Min, the milk cows. Two of their best horses were tethered to the back of the wagon where Aunt Clara was sitting. Ben and Eli climbed up on the seat of that wagon and waited. Aunt Clara had been right about one thing—Luanna was going to walk.

"Until you get tired," her mother had promised. Luanna intended to get tired very quickly.

"Well," Mr. Hamilton said, "I guess this is it. We're to meet the Douglases and the Crawfords out by the Low Pond south of town. Might as well get moving." He cracked his whip high over the animal's heads. "Gee! Haw!" he shouted. The oxen strained at their yokes, and the wagons moved slowly forward.

Luanna stood in the rising dust and looked around her. It was really happening. All her wishing hadn't stopped this day from coming. It seemed to her that her world stood still—her real world—Midford Falls. Only the wagons moved slowly away, leaving her behind.

"Luanna! Luanna!" It was Nancy, running through the tamarack trees into the clearing and around the side of the house. "Oh, Luanna, I had to come to say good-bye again."

Luanna felt Nancy's arms around her. She heard her voice. But none of it seemed real. "Look, Lu, I've brought you a diary. It's just a little one, but you can write in it every night. When you come back home, we can read it together! Oh . . . Lu!"

A tear from Nancy's cheek fell on Luanna's hand. It felt warm and wet. It felt real. This was good-bye, Luanna thought. There wasn't anything she could do to change it. Her own tears mixed with Nancy's. "I have to go now," she said softly. "But I'll be back, Nance. I'll be back some-day."

She looked once at the house. It was Aunt Prue's house now. Then she turned and walked along the still-dusty road behind the wagons.

Four

It didn't take Luanna long to learn about bringing up the rear. The dust rose in thick brown clouds, stirred by wagon wheels and shuffling hoofs. It settled in her hair and on her clothes and made her skin feel gritty. When she reached up to wipe away the tears that were still on her cheeks, her fingers came away streaked with mud.

Aunt Clara sat in the back of the end wagon looking out at Luanna from between Pa's two good horses. She didn't look the least bit uncomfortable to Luanna, but with Aunt Clara you could never tell.

As soon as they reached the sloping pasture of Long Meadow, Luanna left the road and walked along in the short spring grass. Even here, the dust swirled, lifting quickly on the early morning breeze before it settled slowly, powdering the green countryside with a thin layer of brown dirt.

The Douglases were already waiting at the edge of Low Pond. Ian waved when he saw them coming and started across the field to talk to Ben. Ian was sixteen, but Luanna thought he seemed older. Maybe it was because he was always so serious. She watched him as he walked, noticing how tall he had become. Tall and slim, but broad in the shoulders, and with a purposeful air about him. Ian was already a man, she thought, while her brother Ben was still a boy. An unfamiliar tingle touched the base of Luanna's spine. She had known Ian Douglas all her life, and now she suddenly wondered if she knew him at all.

Amy, Ian's sister, was only twelve, and she was just the opposite of her brother, always laughing and ready for fun. Luanna wondered how she managed to stay so cheerful, with her mother dead just one year and only old Mrs. Tatum coming in a few times a week to help with the cooking and housework. Responsibility didn't seem to dampen Amy's spirit. She came running up to Luanna now, her bonnet hanging loose and wisps of sandy hair already escaping from the two thick braids that she always wore.

"Pa's had us up since before the sun," she exclaimed. "Seem's like he can't wait to get started. And now he's fit to be tied because the Crawfords are late. I told him if he doesn't quit his pacing, he'll wear out his traveling shoes." Amy reached out and touched Luanna's arm. "You ought to walk up front, Lu," she said. "That's what I'm going to do. It's better than getting all that dust in your eyes."

Luanna nodded, but she didn't answer. She couldn't trust herself to speak to anybody. Not yet.

There was a clattering along the road that led down by the river, and the Crawford wagon came into view. It was a ramshackle sight, pulled by two yoke of scruffy oxen and with the canvas hood already leaning to one side. The one milk cow looked sickly, and two hungry-looking dogs trotted along with their ears laid back. Luanna didn't wonder. The pots and pans had been tied to the back of the wagon like afterthoughts, and they banged and crashed as the wagon swayed.

As the Crawfords drew closer, Luanna heard her father

exclaim, "Look at that, Jeremy. Their water barrels are already leaking a steady stream."

"No more'n what you'd expect," Jeremy Douglas answered.

Tyler Crawford and his wife, Nab, were sitting on the raised seat up front. Nab took up most of the room because she was so fat. Luanna had heard Aunt Clara say once that it would take a whole bolt of material to go around her. Luanna could see two other little Crawford heads in the wagon, peering out from behind their parents. Belvidry came walking along one side of the oxen and her older brother, Tawny, along the other. He held a whip in one hand. When he saw they were all watching, he swung it over his head and cracked it hard, making the air snap with the sound.

"I'd almost forgotten," Amy whispered, "how much I don't like Tawny Crawford."

Luanna nodded. "He's worse than Belvidry," she said. He was a lot worse, and she made a point of staying as far away from him as she could. At least, she had until now.

Tyler Crawford pulled his oxen straight along the road until he was well in front of the other wagons. Then he climbed down from his seat and ambled back to talk to Mr. Hamilton and Jeremy Douglas. Belvidry was right behind him, but when he stopped she kept on coming. " 'Morning, Lu," she said. She didn't speak to Amy at all, and Luanna knew why. It was because Amy's brother, Ian, didn't have the time of day for Belvidry Crawford and had told her to quit bothering him.

But Amy wasn't easy to ignore. "You look pretty happy, Belvidry," she said. "Aren't you sorry to be leaving Midford Falls?"

"Midford Falls!" Belvidry made a spitting sound. "What's this place ever done for me?" She glanced back over her shoulder to see who might be listening. Then she looked right at Luanna. "My pa says that out West things are different. Your name don't matter. It's what you do that counts. That means once we leave this town, we all start out even. It's no more Hamilton and Crawford and who lives in the biggest house. It's just plain Luanna and Belvidry. We'll see who comes out on top. We'll just see!"

"Move out!" came the call. It was Jeremy Douglas's voice, but the Crawford wagon was in the lead, already rolling, stirring up the dust that had just started to settle.

Belvidry looked pleased. "We're the lead wagon," she said.

Amy grinned. "You'd better enjoy it today. My pa says we all take turns. That means you'll be tail end tomorrow."

Belvidry turned and stalked away, flipping her skirts from side to side the way she always did. "You've made her mad," Luanna warned.

Amy shrugged. "Ian says Belvidry was born mad. I can't help that. Come on, Lu. If we have to walk, we might as well find a better place to do it."

Luanna had traveled this road before. She and Nancy had ridden in the back of the wagon once when Mr. Hamilton had business in Bridport, ten miles to the west. It had been a little bumpy, but it hadn't seemed so far. Things were different, she thought, when you traveled with your feet on the ground. The grassy fields and rolling hills seemed to spread away until they became a gray haze on the horizon, and the more you walked, the farther the horizon stretched out of sight.

She and Amy kept well to the side of the road to avoid the dust. The first few miles weren't so bad. The sun was still low in the sky, and the morning breezes were cool on their skins. The meadows were thick with new grass and spotted with patches of red clover. The chestnut trees spread their branches wide, and sometimes the air was sweet with the smell of pines from the hills.

It wasn't long before Emmie joined them. "I don't like it up in the wagon," she said. "It makes me feel sick." Luanna saw the way the wagons lurched when the wheels struck ruts and swayed even when the road was smooth. It almost made her sick just to watch. She took Emmie by the hand. "It's better here," she said. "Look, we can even have a wild-flower hunt." But Luanna's legs were getting tired, and she really didn't feel like doing anything more than sitting down to rest.

When they came to the banks of Lemon Creek, a little stream that trickled down from Snake Mountain, they took off their shoes and stockings and waded across. Luanna thought creek water had never felt so good.

"We're halfway to Bridport already," Mr. Hamilton called out. "We're making fine time."

Halfway to Bridport! That meant they had come only five miles. Luanna tried not to think about how far it was to California. She was almost sure she was getting a blister on her toe.

At noon they stopped in the shade of a pine grove and ate the lunch that Luanna's mother had packed the night before. There was chicken, ham, dried apples, and fresh bread, but Luanna had swallowed so much dust she couldn't seem to taste a thing. When they started off again, Amy decided to ride for a while, and Emmie went so fast asleep that Mr. Hamilton had to pick her up and carry her to the wagon. Luanna wished she could be picked up and carried, too. She would get on one of her father's horses and ride it, except he had said so much about not wearing out the stock.

Bridport was ahead. They passed right through it, and then it was behind. Luanna wondered if this was the way it was going to be—wait to get somewhere, and then leave it behind you—all the way to California.

The crack of a whip split the air. Tawny Crawford had been doing that all morning. Luanna had half a mind to tell him what she thought. "Crazy thing!" she muttered.

"Who are you talking to?" It was Aunt Clara, leaning out to look at her from the back of the wagon. Her mouth was all pursed up with the kind of look she had when she was about to swat a fly.

"I'm talking to myself," Luanna snapped. "I think Tawny Crawford must be crazy."

To her amazement, Aunt Clara nodded her head. "If I was his ma," she said, "I'd break that whip across his backside." She squinted her eyes at Luanna. "Come here, girl. You might as well ride awhile."

Aunt Clara had shuffled around in the wagon enough to make a bigger hole for herself. If she moved as far as she could to one side, there was room for Luanna. Luanna took one look at the cramped quarters and shook her head. She had never been that close to Aunt Clara in her life, and she didn't want to start now.

Aunt Clara raised a finger and shook it in her face. "I'm not asking—I'm telling! This is your first day out. If you don't rest your legs, you'll be good for nothing tomorrow. Now come here."

Luanna clamped her teeth together to keep from answering, sidestepped the horses that were plodding along behind, and eased herself into the space Aunt Clara had made. The first thing she noticed was that the smell of Aunt Clara's lavender toilet water was even stronger than the dust. After that, she noticed the view, because Aunt Clara pointed it out to her.

"I've looked at those horses' faces until I've memorized every hair," she said. "I can tell you right now I've seen better sights."

Luanna nodded. "I have, too," she said, "and they're all behind us." Then she closed her eyes and almost immediately went to sleep with her head on Aunt Clara's bony shoulder.

When she woke, her neck was stiff, and her body felt as if every bone had been jolted out of place. She moaned softly and tried to sit up straight. "I feel sore all over," she complained. "I think I must be coming down with something."

She really did feel sick, and the feeling made her happier than she'd been in days. If she was sick enough, they would have to turn back—at least her family would. They would have to take her home. Luanna leaned her head back against a box and closed her eyes. She could see herself stretched out on her own bed. The doctor was there, looking worried. She saw him shake his head. "Just in time," he was telling her father. "You brought this child home just in time."

The wagon lurched and jolted her upright just as Aunt Clara's raspy voice sounded in her ear. "Poppycock!" she said. "You're no tireder than the rest of us, and you don't look sick to me." Suddenly she reached out and pinched Luanna's chin between her skinny fingers. "Listen to me, girl. You're going west, no matter how you feel. You might as well get used to the idea."

Luanna had never hated Aunt Clara as much as she did then. She stared hard at the wrinkled face. It had beady eyes, she thought. Small, and beady, and—mean. Without a word she jumped from the back of the wagon and began walking as fast as she could. She climbed a hillock above the pasture north of the road and stood alone, looking back the way they had come. She didn't even turn around when she heard footsteps behind her. When Ian Douglas spoke, it seemed that his voice was right in her ear.

"I saw you coming up here," he said. "I thought it might be a good view. But you're looking the wrong way." He shaded his eyes and pointed in the opposite direction along the crest of the road westward to where a blue ribbon of water shone in the late afternoon sun.

She watched him take off his hat and wipe his forehead with the back of his shirt sleeve. He was dusty all over. Luanna thought if somebody swatted him it would be just like beating a dirty rug. But when he put one hand on her shoulder and leaned forward to show her where to look, she didn't move away. "It's Lake Champlain," he said. "We'll camp near the banks tonight and head south in the morning." He looked down at her. "You really minded leaving, didn't you?"

"I still do."

"I kind of hated it myself, but I wouldn't turn back now for anything." His hand tightened on her shoulder. "It's a whole new world waiting for us—like nothing we've ever seen before."

"I liked the one we had," she told him.

He nodded. "But we can't go back, can we?"

She was just about to tell him that that's exactly what she intended to do the first chance she got when the sound of Tawny Crawford's whip cracked like a gunshot in the distance. Luanna looked toward the Crawford's wagon. There he was, standing by the side of the road, staring up at the hillock where she and Ian stood. It gave her an uneasy feeling to have him watching like that. Almost as if he were waiting for her to do something she shouldn't.

"Stay away from him, Lu." Ian's voice sounded tight, as if it had caught in his throat.

"I always do."

Ian shook his head. "You mean you always have. It'll be harder now that we're all traveling together. Tawny Crawford means trouble. He takes it with him wherever he goes."

As they walked together down the slope of the meadow toward the dusty road, Luanna caught sight of Belvidry, walking along slowly, all by herself. For a second she felt sorry for her, just because she had Tawny for a brother.

Then she remembered what Belvidry had said about starting off even—and about seeing who would come out on
top. Luanna decided right then she was going to stay away
from Belvidry Crawford just the way she stayed away from
Tawny. And she wasn't going to feel sorry for either one of
them. Not in a million years.

Five

Luanna would always associate that first night with the smell of fresh fish cooking over an open fire. "There's plenty more in the lake," Mr. Hamilton said. "We'll eat from the land like this whenever we can and save our supplies until we need them." He looked meaningfully toward Tyler Crawford's wagon where Mrs. Crawford was cooking bacon because neither Mr. Crawford nor Tawny had wanted to bother catching fish. "I swear," he muttered, "those people never think two days ahead."

Luanna thought he must be right. Her mother had shown her how to skim the rich cream from the milk at night and put it into the churn that hung under the wagon. It sloshed around all day on the trail, and there was fresh butter for dinner. One time Belvidry had been standing off to the side watching. "My ma says we'll worry about making butter after we run out of what we brought with us," she said.

"Fine and dandy," Luanna retorted. "Just don't come around borrowing any from us."

After the supper things were cleared away and the tents

set up, Luanna found the diary that Nancy had given her and one of Miss Wilson's pens and some ink. *The first day is over,* she wrote. *I have blisters on my feet, and I am lonesome for home.*

Luanna sat a moment, remembering how Nancy had thought it would be so exciting to go west. She wondered how Nancy would feel now with blisters, and tired legs, and sunburn on her arms and the back of her neck. Nancy had said to write in the diary every night so they could read it together when Luanna came home. But there hadn't been anything strange or wonderful to write about —at least not yet.

Luanna sighed. She didn't even have enough imagination left to make anything up. The best she could do, she thought, was to describe things the way she saw them. She picked up the pen and began to tell about the lake, the clearing, and the sounds of a tired camp. *I can see the lake through the trees,* she wrote,

all shimmery and tipped with silver. The breeze is fresh and cool. Pa keeps saying how fine it is to be camping out like this, but I keep thinking it will be a long time before I sleep in a bed again. Mr. Douglas is singing a soft song, and I can hear Amy humming along. The supper fires are burning low, and nobody is talking much, except for Nathaniel, and he can't seem to stop. Mother keeps reminding me he's only seven.

When she couldn't think of anything more to say, she closed the little book and put it back into the memory box. There ought to be something else in there, she thought, to remind her of the first night of the journey—something she could show Nancy when she saw her again.

Luanna slipped around the back of the end wagon and began walking toward the lake shore. The moon was bright and full, and she could easily see her way. At the water's edge she knelt where smooth pebbles were embedded in the wet soil. One stone seemed to catch the moon's rays and toss them back. She pried it loose and held it in the palm of her hand. It was a smooth, egg-shaped stone that was as white as milk and felt like satin when she rubbed it between her fingers. There was no roughness on it anywhere, and it made her feel good just to hold it against her skin. After a few moments, she got to her feet and made her way quickly back to the campfire. She put the pebble into the box and told herself that the moon shining overhead was also shining over Midford Falls. Home was only a day's walk away.

She held that thought in her mind as she lay in the tent with her eyes wide open, listening to the sounds of voices murmuring late into the night.

Midford Falls seemed farther away in the morning when the wagons pulled out. They headed south along the lake into the Champlain Lowlands, rich with apple orchards and level fields of wheat. Even though the cool spring air was refreshing, Luanna felt heavy-hearted. She knew that they would soon be leaving familiar sights.

A few days later they left Vermont, crossing over into the woodlands of New York in the middle of a rain that drenched the countryside and sent everybody to the wagons and whatever crowded shelter they could find. It rained on and off for several days. "We can't let a little thing like this slow us down," Mr. Hamilton said. "These are just showers. They'll help to clear the air."

So they sloshed along until the puddles dried, following the Champlain Canal and the busy Hudson River, where they could see the steamboats that carried passengers and freight. They had been traveling nine days when they reached the great falls at Cohoes and the break in the Appalachian Mountains at the valley where the Hudson

River met the Mohawk. The blisters got worse, and then they got better. Belvidry claimed not to have any, but Luanna could see plain as day that she was limping.

"I wonder why she lies about it," she said to Amy one day.

"I don't think she can help it," Amy told her. "Anyway, it's more like pretending than lying. Belvidry always has to pretend things are better than they are."

Luanna thought there might be something to that. With a brother like Tawny Crawford, it would be awfully hard to face the truth.

It was the middle of May by the time they turned west into the sparsely settled Mohawk River Valley. The Erie Canal followed the course of the Mohawk River, and this was to be their route. They kept to the towpath side of the canal, sometimes using the same hard-packed path where the horses and mules hauled the canal boats through the water. But when traffic on the canal was heavy and the path too narrow, the wagons had to pull off and travel along one of the old winding trails that led through the valley.

"We're going to take our time," Mr. Hamilton kept promising. "There's no need to hurry. We'll just meander along and enjoy the scenery. It'll be a vacation, like I promised."

Luanna couldn't see that it was much of a vacation for anybody. Up at dawn, cooking over a campfire, walking until your legs about dropped off, swallowing enough dust to choke a horse, then falling onto bedrolls every night so you'd be rested enough to do the same thing tomorrow. She had to admit that every third day things were a little better. That was when the Hamilton wagons were first in line and the dust was behind them.

On those days Luanna walked up front as far as she could, and Amy usually came along. Emmie joined them whenever she felt sick from riding in the wagon. Nathaniel and Tink were always nearby, trying to keep track of the animals, and Ben and Eli often took turns stretching their legs. The best times were when they all got together and shouted "halloos" to the canalboats passing by.

There were wide-bottomed flatboats carrying freight, and passenger packets carrying travelers who sat on the cabin roofs and had to duck their heads whenever they came to a bridge. There were rafts that drifted slowly along and managed to get in everybody's way, and little shanty boats with people living in them. Luanna thought they looked like broken-down shacks floating on the water. Sometimes there were boats carrying entire families and all their belongings.

"I wish we could travel like that," said Luanna. She sat down in the soft grass by the side of the towpath and took off her shoes.

"I reckon we could if we wanted to leave the wagons behind," Amy answered. "But we'd just have to buy other wagons for the rest of the trip. My pa says we'd best count pennies. It's a long way yet to California."

Luanna couldn't let herself think about how far it was. If she started measuring the miles in her mind, she got more homesick than ever. Instead, she tried keeping track of the things she could write about in her diary each night— things that might seem exciting to Nancy.

She wrote about watching the boats entering the locks, where the water was raised or lowered to new levels so they could continue on their way. At Little Falls, there were five locks, like giant steps, and a big aqueduct where the water carried the boats high in the air as if they were on a bridge.

When the wagons rounded a bend, Luanna could see the town of Little Falls. *I caught my breath*, she wrote that night. *For a moment I thought I was home again. The houses*

*were spread out against the hillside, and the church spire was
pointed and white, just like at Midford Falls. But we didn't
even stop, and the place was soon behind us.*

She tried to describe the steersmen and the way they
lifted their long, slender horns to the sky and blew warning notes to other boats; the towpath walkers, who pa-
trolled back and forth along a ten-mile stretch, looking
for breaks in the canal and stuffing holes with straw and
clay; and the young boys called "hoggees," who drove the
horses and mules that pulled the boats along the canal and
shouted "Haw!" and "Gee!" in voices that carried over the
water.

At night the towpath became a racecourse, and excited
shouts filled the air as young men on horses galloped past.
But on the canal the traffic went on, even after dark, when
bow lamps from the boats cast an eerie sheen upon the
water.

There were taverns and inns along the way, and sometimes the canal went right through towns. But the Hamiltons and Douglases didn't stop. "We have everything we
need in our own wagons," Mr. Hamilton said proudly.

Tyler Crawford had different ideas. He often stopped off
at one of the taverns, leaving his wife and Tawny to
manage on their own. He always caught up later, hurrying
along behind the wagons in a stumbling gait that took him
from one side of the road to the other.

"You mark my word," Jeremy Douglas said. "He'll be
turning his pockets inside out before we reach Illinois. I tell
you, Daniel, I'm already sorry he came with us."

The next morning, the Crawford milk cow fell in the
canal and drowned. "Nobody was watching the poor
skinny thing," Mr. Hamilton said. "I guess it wanted a
drink of water. Got tangled up in a tow rope and went
over sideways."

Tyler Crawford was under the weather and couldn't be

bothered with cows. "Leave her float," he muttered. "Not enough meat on her to butcher anyway." But that night, when he was feeling better, he blamed Tawny for the whole thing. "Nobody in this family tends to business!" he shouted. He would have whipped him right there, but Tawny was quick to get out of the way. The last Luanna saw of him, Tawny was disappearing into the woods.

Then Mr. Crawford turned on his wife. "What are we going to do without a milk cow?" he demanded.

Nab Crawford didn't answer, just climbed into the wagon and pulled the flap down behind her, and that's where she stayed. She didn't even come out when Tawny came sneaking back or when the wagons rolled in the morning.

Nobody knew if she was sick or just mad until the next night when Mrs. Hamilton decided she'd better go over there and see. She came back looking worried. "Nab's not well, Daniel. Her color's bad, and she can hardly talk without coughing. I think she should see a doctor, but Tyler won't hear of it. He says he doesn't have spare cash for foolishness.

Luanna didn't see much of Belvidry these days. Belvidry had to do all the cooking and washing for the Crawfords, so she didn't have time to come poking around where she wasn't wanted. "She's got her hands full," Amy said, "what with her mother sick and two little ones to tend to. That brother of hers won't lift a hand to help."

Luanna looked at Tawny leaning against the side of the wagon, watching Belvidry work. He glanced quickly over his shoulder and shifted his weight restlessly. Tawny has an unquiet look about him, Luanna thought, as if he is always waiting for something to happen.

"I guess he spends all the energy he's got keeping out of his pa's way," she told Amy.

It was early in June and the sun was warm. They followed the canal beside the Niagara River until it emptied into Lake Erie near Buffalo. "We'll work our way around the lake shore," Mr. Hamilton said, "and in a couple of weeks we'll pick up the Ohio Canal and follow it right down to the National Road."

Luanna thought Lake Erie looked like a great sea. She hadn't expected anything so immense, with blue water as far as she could see. A broad, sandy beach stretched along the shoreline, and a gentle breeze cooled the air. The water was fresh and clean and so full of fish that they feasted on it every night. Luanna learned to roast whitefish over an open fire, fry it in a pan, or boil it in the kettle with onions and potatoes.

They didn't try to make many miles in a day. "It's so lovely," Luanna's mother said. "I wish we could stay a while." Everyone agreed, so they did stay a few days in one spot. It was wonderful, Luanna thought, to be able to walk barefoot in the sand and let the tiny waves lap at your toes. One day she took her diary with her and sat at the edge of the lake with it. *Oh, Nance*, she wrote, *how you would love it here! I never dreamed of such a lake. I think it must be as big as an ocean, and the water is bluer than the sky.*

She heard a sound behind her and turned quickly, covering the page with her hand.

"You won't find any seashells here." It was Tawny Crawford. She wondered how long he had been standing there watching her.

"I—I wasn't looking for any."

He came closer and squinted at the diary. "I see you writin' in that thing a lot." He held out his hand. "Let me see."

Luanna got up so quickly that the ink bottle tipped and splattered a dark stain across one page. "Now look what you've made me do!" she snapped. She looked at Tawny and was sorry she had spoken. His little eyes narrowed, and his thin lips pulled into two hard, straight lines.

He took a step closer. "Give it to me," he said. He looked

like a weasel, Luanna thought. She didn't want him coming any closer.

"You stop right there, Tawny Crawford. I'm not giving you this diary, so you can forget about it right now." She brushed the sand from her skirt and deliberately turned away from him and started back toward the wagons. "I have things to do," she said. "I'm surprised you don't."

When she felt his hand on her arm, she whirled angrily. "Leave me alone!" she ordered. Tawny laughed. It was a high, silly sound that trailed along the sand and across the water. He stepped forward and reached for her again. "What's the matter?" he asked. "You been writin' secrets in your little book?"

Luanna backed away slowly, but he kept on coming. "You got nowhere to run," he told her, "where I can't catch you."

She felt the bottle of ink in her hand. The lid was still loose. She unscrewed it quickly. "One more step, Tawny," she threatened. He laughed again and lunged forward, grabbing for the diary. The ink splashed across his face and hair, running down the front of his shirt. He reached up to feel the wetness of it, then stared at his hands.

"I'll get you for this," he promised. "Just you wait! First chance I get, I'll—"

"You'll what, Tawny?" It was Ben's voice. Luanna's brother was walking toward them, coming from the camp. When he got a good look at Tawny, he grinned. "Looks to me like you'd better have a bath."

Tawny looked at Ben and began moving away. "You don't scare me none," he muttered. "None at all." Then he turned and broke into a trot, leaving his footprints in the sand.

Ben put his arm around Luanna. "Are you all right? What was he up to, anyway?"

To Luanna's horror, tears cascaded down her cheeks.

"Oh, Lu, don't do that," Ben soothed. "Come on with me back to the wagons. Don't worry. I'll see that he keeps away from you from now on."

"I—I'm not afraid of him," Luanna insisted.

"Of course you're not." Ben patted her gently on the back. "But I'm afraid he doesn't think too highly of you right now."

Luanna allowed herself to be led back to the wagons after she had washed her face in the lake. It was no use explaining why she was crying. Nobody would understand. But all Luanna could think about for the rest of the evening was that she had thrown almost a whole bottle of ink on Tawny Crawford. A whole precious bottle of Miss Wilson's ink was gone.

Six

Luanna thought if she never ate whitefish again it would be too soon. At first it had tasted fine, but three weeks later, by the time the wagons left the lake at Cleveland and turned south along the steep, wooded bluffs of the Cuyahoga River, she was sick to death of it.

"You're an ungrateful girl," Aunt Clara scolded. "It's a sin to turn up your nose at what the Lord provides."

Luanna believed the Lord provided a variety so people could have a choice, but she had better sense than to say so. Aunt Clara was on the warpath as it was, carrying on about Luanna's mother working her fingers to the bone for that ungrateful passel of Crawfords.

"A lot of thanks you'll get for your trouble," she snapped one evening, as Mrs. Hamilton prepared a poultice for Nab Crawford.

Mrs. Hamilton went right on chopping onions. For several nights now she had fried them in a pan to get them good and hot, then carried them over to the Crawford wagon where she would layer them between steaming cloths on Mrs. Crawford's chest. Luanna took a sniff and was glad she wasn't the one who had a cough. People could smell the fumes clear across the camp. She couldn't imagine what it would be like to have all those onions in her wagon with the flap pulled down, and she felt more than a little sorry for Mrs. Crawford.

After a while, Luanna's mother put the pan aside and wiped her streaming eyes. "I'm not asking for thanks," she said. "I just wish Nab would show some improvement. She needs to see a doctor, but Tyler says . . ."

Everybody knew what Tyler Crawford said. He couldn't afford a doctor—didn't need one—wouldn't have one poking around his wagon. But he sure didn't mind complaining. It seemed to Luanna that he hadn't done much else since Mrs. Crawford came down sick.

"I'm sure tired of hearing about how bad off the Crawfords are," Luanna told Amy. Then she looked around to see if anyone was listening. "First I lose my fine milk cow, and now my poor, dear wife is ailing," she mimicked in a high, whining voice.

Amy giggled. "Oh, Lu, that's just like he sounds. My pa says Mr. Crawford's just as glad the cow fell in and drowned because now he doesn't have to bother to milk her. And it looks like he isn't worrying himself about food either. Whenever his family is hungry or thirsty, he takes all he needs from the rest of us."

Luanna nodded. "I know. He was at our wagon last night."

The memory was all too clear. "Look here, Daniel," Luanna had heard Tyler Crawford say. He had his hat in his hands, his voice purred like the old gray tomcat Luanna had left behind in Midford Falls. "I'm running a little low on supplies. If you folks can see your way clear to share a little, I'll never forget your kindness." He sniffed loudly and wiped a dirty shirt sleeve across dry eyes. "How's a man to manage along the trail without a good woman to help him?"

Mr. Hamilton fixed him up with some beans and gave him precious sugar and a little coffee. "You should have eaten fish with the rest of us, Tyler. There was plenty in the lake back there."

Tyler hung his head low. "I wasn't thinkin'," he mumbled. "So worried about my dear wife and all . . ."

Aunt Clara gave a snort that could be heard on both sides of the Ohio Canal. "If you're so worried," she demanded, "why don't you get a doctor? You could have found one in Cleveland for sure."

Tyler gave her a tight-lipped smile. "No need for spendin' good money. Miz Hamilton is as good as any doctor I ever seen. She's takin' right good care of my missus." He kept on smiling and nodding until he got the food across the clearing into his own camp. Then they heard his voice raised in anger. "You're a worthless crew!" he shouted. "A bunch of lazy good-for-nothings! Look here at this food I brought. Don't just stand there lettin' your toenails grow, Belvidry. Get these beans in the cookin' pot!"

Luanna shook her head, still remembering. "Mr. Crawford's a selfish man," she told Amy.

Amy looked at her and laughed. "Selfish nothing! My pa says he isn't fit for the dirt he walks on."

The next day was Sunday. "You mark my word," Aunt Clara said. "Tyler Crawford won't want to budge. He always gets religion when it gives him a chance to rest." Sure enough, Mr. Crawford refused to pull out in the morning.

"It's the Lord's Day," he intoned. "Don't nobody expect me to travel on a day like this."

Luanna was surprised when her mother was the one who stood up to him this time. "We always try to stop on Sundays," she reminded him, "but this time we need to move on—at least until we find a settlement big enough to support a doctor. Nab's worse, Tyler—she really is. I've treated her the best I know how, but she doesn't get any better. She's coughing something awful. Sometimes she can hardly get her breath."

Tyler's eyes narrowed. "You're the one been takin' care of her. If anything happens, it'll be your fault."

Luanna guessed if her father had been listening, Tyler Crawford wouldn't have felt like going anywhere for several days, let alone Sunday. As it was, Aunt Clara spoke up.

"You listen to me," she commanded. "Rebecca Hamilton has done about all she's going to do for you and your family. It's one thing to help out a neighbor in trouble—and another to put up with the likes of you. You've got four children over there, and you haven't lifted a hand to help one of them. All you care about is yourself and your bottle." Aunt Clara reached out with her pipe and shook it under Tyler's nose. "If Nab dies, the shame's on you."

Mr. Crawford began to mutter, but he went and yoked up his oxen anyway. When the other two families broke camp and started across the fields toward the towpath, he followed right along. Tawny sat on the raised seat beside him, and Belvidry brought up the rear, walking with the young ones in the rising dust.

The Ohio Canal followed the old traders' route upstream along the Cuyahoga River as far as Akron, Ohio, then across the overland trail and downstream along the tributaries that drained to the great Ohio River. When they reached Akron, they stopped in a clearing at the edge of the woods and, despite Mr. Crawford's protests, Jeremy Douglas and Mr. Hamilton set out to find a doctor.

"This is a fair-sized city," Luanna's father said. "There are bound to be trained men here."

The one they brought back was a tall, rangy fellow who looked more like a backwoodsman than a professional doctor. He swung along across the clearing to where the three families had set up camp alongside a stream. His black bag seemed too small for the rest of him, but his eyes were bright and friendly, and Luanna liked the looks of his hands—like her father's, somehow, both strong and gentle.

He disappeared into the Crawfords' wagon and took Becky Hamilton with him. It seemed to Luanna that they stayed in there a long time. "What do you suppose they're doing?" she whispered to Amy.

Amy shook her head. "I don't know much about doctoring," she said. "I sure wish I did. It's really awful, Lu, when somebody gets sicker and sicker, and there isn't anything you can do about it."

Luanna remembered that Amy's mother had been dead for just a little over a year. She couldn't imagine what it would be like to have her mother die. She looked over at the Crawford wagon and saw Belvidry bending over the two youngest Crawfords. By the way they were squirming, Luanna decided she must be washing their faces. It was a good thing, too. Maybe people could tell them apart if they got the dirt off and their noses wiped.

Belvidry seemed to have heard the two girls talking, for she straightened up all of a sudden and looked over her shoulder at them. Luanna had never seen Belvidry look that way before—her eyes open wide and the skin on her face stretched tight. There was only one way to describe it. Belvidry Crawford looked scared.

When the wagon flap opened and the doctor came out, Belvidry stared at him, but she didn't say a word, just pulled the little ones back out of the way. Luanna could see Tawny skulking around by the back of the wagon, looking as if he didn't want to be there at all.

"Well, you sure did take your time!" Mr. Crawford's voice had an edge to it. "You must have fixed her up better'n new." Then, before the doctor had a chance to answer, "Say, doc, mebbe you had ought to have a look at my back. It's been botherin' me somethin' awful. 'Course I try to do my share of the heavy work, and that's—"

The doctor took him by the arm and steered him off to one side where nobody could hear what he had to say. He spoke in a low voice that was interrupted by Tyler Crawford's angry exclamations.

"What do you mean by that, mister? I don't believe a word of it. You don't have no call to upset me this way!" And then, shaking his fist, "You'd best take your black bag and get out of my sight. I didn't want you here in the first place."

The wagon flap opened again, and Luanna's mother climbed out. Her face looked drained, and there were lines around her mouth and eyes. Mr. Crawford's words had attracted a lot of attention. Tawny was nowhere in sight, but everybody else in the camp had gathered round, trying to hear what was going on and at the same time look as if they weren't listening. Mrs. Hamilton went over to Belvidry and put her arm around her.

"Oh, dear," whispered Amy. "I'm afraid . . ."

Luanna was afraid too, and she didn't exactly know why. The Crawfords weren't her family. She didn't care what happened to a single one of them. She watched Belvidry standing stiff in the half circle of Rebecca Hamilton's arm.

The doctor turned and walked away from Mr. Crawford. He stopped in front of Belvidry, reached out, and put his hand on her shoulder. "I'm sorry," he said. "There isn't anything I can do." Then he nodded to Mr. Hamilton and Jeremy Douglas and left the camp. Luanna thought he looked sad—and he didn't know the Crawfords at all!

Tyler Crawford climbed into his wagon—and climbed right out again, carrying a bottle in one hand. He walked over to where Luanna's mother still stood with her arm tight around Belvidry. Luanna noticed her father walking quickly toward them. He got there just as Mr. Crawford raised his arm and pointed a finger at her mother.

"You!" he said. "It's your fault that my wife's dying."

Mr. Hamilton's hand closed over Tyler Crawford's arm. "Don't talk foolish," he said. "The doctor said nothing could have saved her. She must have been sick even before we left Midford Falls."

Mr. Crawford backed away and turned around a couple of times, as if he wasn't sure which way to go. Then he headed straight for the woods and disappeared.

That night there was a screech owl in the trees. It started crying soon after the sun went down. "It's bad luck," Belvidry whispered to no one in particular. She went over and sat near her own campfire, shivering, even though the air was warm. After a bit, she got one of her mother's aprons and began tying knots in it to make the screech owl stop.

"That's foolishness," Luanna said, watching her. "Anybody with any sense knows that old trick doesn't work. Besides, we've heard screech owls lots of times, and nobody said anything about bad luck before."

"Leave her be, child." Aunt Clara puffed her pipe slowly, sending little whirls of blue smoke into the air. "It gives her something to do."

Nab Crawford died before the moon was high. Mrs. Hamilton brought Belvidry and the young ones over to the Hamilton wagons to spend the night. It was fine weather, and everyone but Aunt Clara slept out where they could see the stars. Luanna thought Belvidry must have watched them all night because every time she looked over at her, her eyes were wide open and staring straight up. Luanna closed her own eyes again and again, but she couldn't sleep either. She figured it was because the screech owl went on crying until morning.

Daniel Hamilton and Jeremy Douglas dug Mrs. Crawford's grave. No one had seen Tyler Crawford since the night before, and Tawny just stood aside and watched.

Nab Crawford was wrapped in a blanket and buried in the ground. Ian climbed up on one of his father's wagons and drove it back and forth across the grave, packing the earth hard before the spot was covered with a mound of rocks. Ben made a marker and stuck the post deep into the ground.

Abigail Crawford, it said. *1816–1851.*

Luanna swallowed hard when she saw it. She wondered how many people knew that Nab Crawford's real name was Abigail—or how many people cared. She looked across the rocky grave to where Belvidry and Tawny were standing. Tawny kept looking over his shoulder as if he wasn't quite sure when his father might reappear. Belvidry stared straight ahead, not looking at much of anything. The two young ones were playing near the wagon. For all the mourning that was going on, Luanna figured Nab Crawford might as well have been a stranger—a fat woman who rode up front on the Crawford wagon and always looked tired.

Mr. Hamilton said a few words over the grave. He had just finished the prayer when there was a commotion near the edge of the woods and Tyler Crawford appeared. "Here now!" he said. "Did you start without me?" Then he fell on his face.

Luanna stood still with the others, waiting for something to happen. Tyler Crawford didn't move. After a moment, Belvidry gave Tawny a nudge, and they walked over to him, each trying to lift him by a shoulder. Ian and Ben moved quickly and helped carry him to the wagon.

Taking care of the living, Luanna thought. But there had been no one to cry for poor Nab. She looked from face to face, seeing sadness, but no grief. Then a lump rose in her throat when she saw Belvidry coming back from the wagon.

Belvidry's face was streaked with tears.

Seven

Tawny Crawford had to do all the driving by himself, now that Mrs. Crawford was gone and Mr. Crawford spent most of his days sleeping off the effects of his drinking. Belvidry was left with the cooking, the washing, and the young ones. She had taken care of the children while her mother was sick, and she knew how to boil a pot of beans and bake bread, but as far as Luanna knew, nobody in the Crawford family had ever washed much of anything. Up to now, that is.

"If that family is going to travel with us all the way to California," Luanna's mother said one night, "they're going to have to change their ways." The next thing Luanna knew, Mrs. Hamilton had collected Belvidry and the young ones and was washing their hair. "Why, Belvidry," her mother exclaimed, "look how pretty and shiny it is when it's clean."

Luanna didn't see anything pretty about the color of dishwater, but she had to admit it had a shine to it. She knew her mother wouldn't be satisfied with just the hair, and it wasn't long before the Crawford clothes were boiling in a big pot of soapy water over a hickory fire. It was just a step from cleanliness to cooking, and by the time the wagons had traveled south as far as Coshocton, Ohio, Belvidry had learned there was more to eating than a plate of beans. She had even gotten Tawny to catch a few fish and shoot a squirrel or two.

Luanna supposed all that was well and good. What bothered her was that Belvidry was underfoot so much of the time. "I got to ask your mother a question," she would say, tossing her head in that irritating way she had. And the young ones were always with her, hanging around like pets waiting to be fed.

Luanna was half-surprised to find out the little ones had names. Alvin was the boy, short and stocky, with big, dark eyes that never blinked. He was way past three, but he'd never yet said a word. The girl was Sally Sue. She was Nathaniel's age, but such a skinny little thing she looked no bigger than Emmie, who was two years younger. Sally Sue had such pale blue eyes there was hardly any color in them at all. *She* could talk—Belvidry said so—but Luanna had never heard her make a sound, exept for coughing and sniffling.

Mrs. Hamilton never complained about them being around. "Belvidry's learning fast," she said. "I have to admire the way she's taking hold. She doesn't seem a bit like Tawny or her father, does she?"

Luanna sighed. Belvidry was going to be with her day after day, whether she liked it or not. There wasn't a thing she could do about it.

It was hot summer now. The Fourth of July came and went without much of a celebration. They would not have celebrated at all, but Tink found some wild honey in an old oak tree when he was looking for a ewe that had wandered off the towpath. "Come on!" he shouted. "We'll smoke those bees out and steal their treasure."

Ben, Eli, and Ian ran to help him. Mrs. Hamilton made Nathaniel stay back a ways because whenever he got stung the welts swelled up something awful. Luanna and Amy watched from a safe distance as the boys found a dead limb with lots of dried brush on the end and lit it. They let it burn a bit, then Ian swung it about until the flames went out and it began to smoke. When he stuck it in the hollow of the tree, the bees poured out in a buzzing cloud. Quick as a wink, Ben dashed in, his hands wrapped in rags, and pulled the comb free. "Yahoo!" he yelled. He plopped the comb in one of Mrs. Hamilton's big cooking pots, picked the pot up by the handle, and ran.

"Nothin' to it," he announced. But Luanna noticed he was rubbing the back of his neck where the bees had landed.

"I should have gone with you," Nathaniel complained, shooting an indignant look at his mother. He rushed over to the pot and was about to dip a finger into the sticky mess when a bee crawled out and stung him on the hand. "If I was gonna get bit anyway," he fretted, "I should've had some of the fun."

The honey tree was a real find for everyone, for the hive was a big one with plenty of comb. Even Aunt Clara got excited. After they'd set up camp in a big apple orchard, Mrs. Hamilton unpacked her moss rose tea set and made a pot of precious black tea with fresh milk and honey.

Later, Mr. Douglas got out his bagpipes and they could hear him playing them as he walked along the towpath. Mr. Crawford said they gave him a headache, but Luanna liked the sounds. She could hardly believe that it was a whole year since the last Fourth of July when Mr. Douglas had marched in the parade. Back then, Midford Falls, Vermont, had seemed like forever.

In the mornings they tried to get an early start, pushing themselves to make good mileage before the sun got high, then taking an extra rest at midday. They followed the Ohio Canal as far as a place called Dresden Junction, then continued south on the winding Muskingum River route toward Zanesville, Ohio, on the National Road. Luanna was grateful for the shade of the great buckeye trees that grew thick along the towpath and the nearby rolling hills.

One day, when she and Amy were walking together, they collected some of the prickly fruit from the buckeye trees. Breaking them open, they discovered large, shiny-brown seeds with pale scars that made them look just like the eyes of a deer. Luanna decided to save two for her memory box to remind her of Ohio.

She was putting them in her pocket when she heard Ian's voice close by. "Here's something more for your collection," he said. "I found it in the woods near the honey tree." His open palm held an arrowhead. The end was chiseled to a sharp point, and Luanna shuddered when she thought what it might have been used for.

"These parts used to be full of Injuns before the government moved them out West," Ian told her. "I'll bet some savages are still around." He grinned. "You reckon they're slipping behind these trees, watching us?"

"Oh, stop it, Ian! You'll have me believing it."

Luanna reached out and took the arrowhead from his hand. As her fingers touched his, she looked up into his eyes and smiled. He was watching her with an expression she wasn't sure about. It made her feel warm all over, as if he had closed both hands around hers.

"Thank you for the arrowhead," she whispered softly.

Ian nodded, then suddenly looked unsure of himself. "I—I've got to be going," he stammered.

Luanna put the arrowhead in her pocket with the buckeye seeds. When she joined the others along the towpath, Amy looked at her curiously. "Your face is flushed, Lu," she said.

Luanna put one hand on her cheek, remembering the way Ian had made her feel. "Well, it is a hot day," she answered. She walked silently beside Amy in the rising dust.

It seemed that each day was hotter than the one before. Whenever Luanna got a chance, she took off her shoes and left the towpath to walk barefoot in the grass. "Your arms will sunburn if you don't keep your sleeves rolled down," Amy warned her. But Luanna didn't care. The air on her skin felt good. If she could have her way, she'd strip off her bonnet and tuck up her skirts, but she supposed Aunt Clara and her mother would scold her.

There was good fishing in the Muskingum River. The boys caught pike and catfish, but when it came time to eat Luanna could hardly put a bite in her mouth and swallow it. "I feel the same way," Amy confided. "Sometimes I think I'm growing fins." Belvidry was the only one who didn't seem to mind, but they decided it was because she was used to a bean diet, and fish was a welcome change.

Occasionally Mrs. Hamilton would stew up a couple of hens that had quit laying, or a rabbit or squirrel shot by one of the boys, but fish was so plentiful Luanna's father said it seemed like a sin not to take advantage. Relief came when one of Mr. Hamilton's merino ewes got kicked by an ox and Ben had to shoot it. They had mutton roasted over the open fire that night, and thick, rich pot stew for several days.

One evening Luanna was looking at the things in her memory box when she felt a prickle down her spine and turned to see Tawny Crawford watching her. How she hated his sly, knowing looks. "What are you doing, following me around?" she demanded.

"I notice Ian Douglas is plenty welcome," he said. " 'Oh, Ian, thank you for the arrowhead,' " he mocked her.

Suddenly Tawny's eyes narrowed, and his lips seemed to curl. Luanna had seen a dog look like that once before it tried to bite a stranger. "Let me tell you somethin', Miss High-and-Mighty. Ian Douglas isn't the only one can find somethin' special for that box of yours."

"Maybe not, Tawny Crawford. But there isn't anything *you* can give me that I want to have. Now get away from this wagon and leave me alone!"

He left, but he was smiling as he turned away. Luanna was amost sure she could hear him laughing all the way to his own wagon.

Daniel Hamilton and Jeremy Douglas were eager to reach the National Road, so they set a steady pace. "It's the best highway in the country," Luanna's father said. "We'll have smooth sailing all the way to Illinois."

They reached the "highway"—if one could call it that—at Zanesville about mid-July. Luanna and Amy stood on the riverbank near the Y-shaped bridge that went over the Muskingum and watched the tumbling water wind its way to the south.

"No more fish—that's my wish," said Amy.

"Oh, you just wait," Luanna told her. "Pa's already talking about stopping a few days by the Scioto River."

On either side of them, stretching east and west, was the road: a thirty-foot-wide strip of crushed rock, packed hard by wagon wheels and hoofs, and a twenty-foot stretch of soft shoulder on each side of that. A great Conestoga freight wagon rattled westward, its wide wheels crunching against the gravel. The driver voiced a gusty "Halloo!"

A farmer crossed the bridge, driving a flock of gobbling wild turkeys before him. Dogs ran along behind a pack train of mules, barking at the heels of the animals. In the distance a stagecoach was approaching, swaying precariously from side to side. As it careened past, Amy and Luanna raced for the soft shoulder, staying well out of the way. Luanna could just make out the words, NATIONAL ROAD STAGE COMPANY, in fancy letters on its side.

"I didn't know it would be like this!" exclaimed Amy. "It almost takes my breath away."

Luanna nodded. All the commotion—the constant shuffling and bustling of people on the move—she had never seen anything like it. "I never thought . . ." she began, and stopped.

All these people! She closed her eyes and listened, and wondered if she heard a kind of rhythm to the sounds. Hoof beats, and voices, and wheels creaking as they rolled —these were the sounds of a country on the move. She felt a stir of excitement, a tingle that she couldn't quite explain. Seeing the National Road this way wasn't at all the same as looking at lines drawn on a map. This was real. It was alive—and exciting. She would write about it in her book that night. It was something Nancy would want to hear about.

There was a big inn at the side of the road, two stories high with attic windows on top. A vine with yellow flowers covered the railing of the wide, shaded porch where a spotted dog sat, wagging its tail. A wagon was drawn up in front. Chickens pecked lazily in the dust, and horses sucked up water from the wooden trough. Beyond the inn were the shops of a blacksmith and a harness maker, and there was a general supply store. Not a real town, to be sure, but it was a beginning. There was something about the scene that made Luanna think of home.

"What were you going to say, Lu? You stopped halfway," Amy said.

Luanna hesitated. "I—I guess I just never thought—that there was life beyond Vermont."

For a second Luanna let herself remember Midford Falls, then she took Amy by the arm and said, "We'd better run, or we'll get left behind."

Eight

Their wagons rolled steadily along the National Road, keeping to the right, for there was plenty of traffic going the other way: farmers driving their cattle and hogs east to the marketplace, stagecoaches carrying passengers, and wagons filled with coal from the Ohio mines and corn from the farms. It seemed to Luanna that everyone was in perpetual motion, stopping only for meals, for the night, or to pay the tolls along the way.

They didn't stop at the Scioto River after all, but pushed right on across Ohio and into Indiana. "We're doing just fine," Daniel Hamilton said. "Making close to twenty-five miles a day. In a couple of weeks we'll be in Illinois, and we can put up a cabin and settle for the winter."

But Luanna couldn't think that far into the future. There was too much to see every single day. At night she wrote in her book about the noisy, bustling life on the road, and she described the great Conestoga wagons with their colorful red wheels, blue bodies, and white canvas tops.

> *The horses are fine and large, with bells fastened to frames on their shoulders and red yarn tassels on their bridles. I wish I could sit on one and ride a spell. Today we stopped and bought potatoes, onions, and corn. The corn was sweet, and Nathaniel ate it until we thought he would burst. Inns and taverns seem to pop up every few miles as if someone planted them there, but Mr. Crawford is the only one from our party who stops.*

Jeremy Douglas said Tyler Crawford would do well to stay in his wagon and mind his business. "That old wagon of his is about to fall apart," Luanna heard him say.

Sure enough, the Crawford wagon broke down before they reached Indianapolis. It happened in the morning, as they were breaking camp. Mr. Crawford had decided to drive for a change. He had just climbed onto the seat, taking the reins from Tawny and giving the oxen a thwack, when the front left wheel rolled off, and the wagon bed hit the ground with a wood-splintering crash. Mr. Crawford picked himself up.

"Now see what you've gone and done!" he roared at Tawny. "Give over that whip you're so fond of and I'll learn you a thing or two!"

Tawny's face was white as he backed away. "I didn't do nothin', Pa! You can't blame me this time."

"The boy's right." It was Jeremy Douglas who had come to see what was going on. "I don't know how your wagon got this far, Tyler. The wheels were squealing when we left Midford Falls. You pull yourself together, and let's see what we can do about it."

Everybody was all packed up to go, but Daniel Hamilton said they might as well unpack and set up camp again. Repairing that wagon wasn't going to be a one-day job. It turned out that the axle was broken, and the wheel was in bad shape. The wooden rim and spokes had shrunk and the iron tire was so loose that when the wheel hit the ground, the whole thing came apart, the tire rolling like a hoop until it hit a big rock and stopped.

"I'll lay you odds Tyler didn't bring along any spare parts," Mr. Douglas muttered. "I don't see how we're going to get that tire to stay on the rim. We need a blacksmith to heat it red-hot, then shrink it down with cold water. We might try soaking the wheel and letting the wood swell, but it's not a sure thing."

Luanna's father shook his head. "We'd best let him use one of our spares for now. He can get the broken one fixed at the next town."

They tossed a coin to see whose spare was to be used, and Jeremy Douglas lost. He unloaded it from the back of his supply wagon and rolled it over to where Tyler Crawford stood scratching his head. "Much obliged, I'm sure," he simpered. "What would a man do without good neighbors like you?"

Of course, as soon as the work started he began complaining about his back, and it wasn't long before he was sitting back advising the others what to do. The wagon had to be unloaded—that took half the day—then lifted up on stumps until it was high enough to take the new wheel. When it was standing steady once again, the men looked over the considerable damage that had been done to the wagon bed itself.

It was three days before they could break camp again, and when they did, there were four families traveling instead of three. A man and a woman, Mr. and Mrs. Tanner, had come up the Shenandoah River from Virginia and joined the National Road clear back at Cumberland, Maryland, where it started. "We'd be pleased if you'd let us ride along with you to Illinois," Isaac Tanner said.

They crossed over the Wabash at Terre Haute, Indiana,

and turned southwest. "For a road that's supposed to be straight, this one sure twists and jogs a lot," Luanna said.

"It's easier to go around a hill than through it," her father told her. "What's important is that the road you take gets you where you're going."

That was true, she supposed, but the farther west this one went, the worse it got. All the heavy traffic had made deep ruts, and the rains had washed out gullies that had never been repaired. The potholes were so bad, the men had to get down and lead the oxen around them. Tree stumps had been left unpulled, and large rocks littered the surface. In places, logs were laid side by side to form a bumpy roadbed that tripped up the oxen and joggled the wagons. As they neared Vandalia, Illinois, the road was only a wide dirt path between rows of trees. Workmen wore slitted metal guards over their eyes as they swung heavy sledges, smashing rocks and making the gray dust rise all around them. Hammer against stone—hammer against stone—and Irish voices raised in laughter and song. These are the sounds of the end of the road, Luanna thought.

They crossed the Kaskaskia River at Vandalia, and a little way out of town found some land for lease where they could raise a few cabins. It was August now, and they were glad to stop. "We've been on the road three months," Mr. Hamilton said. "This is a good place to settle for the winter."

"Not me," said Tyler Crawford. "You can cut trees and camp out here all you like. I'm takin' my family right back into Vandalia. We're havin' a meal that somebody else cooks for a change, and we're sleepin' in real beds!" He puffed on one of the hand-rolled stogies that he'd bought four for a penny from one of the Conestoga drivers.

"Humph!" muttered Aunt Clara as he drove away. "It's

the tavern that's drawing him back to town. Tyler doesn't have enough money for fancy living."

"Do you suppose that's the last we'll see of the Crawfords?" Amy whispered to Luanna. "Maybe they'll like it so well in town, they'll decide to stay."

Jeremy Douglas shook his head. "You watch," he said. "Tyler will be back the minute he's hard up."

"It's not Tyler I'm concerned about," Mrs. Hamilton put in. "It's Belvidry and those young ones."

Luanna wasn't sure about the young ones, but she was quite sure Belvidry Crawford could take care of herself. And she was glad Tawny was gone. "Out of sight—out of mind," she told herself, and pretty soon she stopped thinking about the Crawfords entirely.

There was mail waiting for them at the tavern in Vandalia, brought all the way from Midford Falls by stage. Mr. Hamilton had told folks to write to them there so they'd be sure not to miss their letters. Luanna got three letters from Nancy. She didn't know whether to open them all at once or save them to enjoy a little at a time. In the end, she opened them one after the other, but read them slowly, again and again.

Things had changed, Nancy said, now that Aunt Prue was living in Luanna's house.

> *Nobody wants to go visiting there anymore. I went once, Lu, and when I saw how all your furniture was changed around, I never could go back.*
>
> *Oh, Lu, I wish you were here. I climbed Snake Mountain and looked as far to the west as I could, trying to imagine where you were. How I wish I could follow you. I'll bet you've changed your mind by now and don't want to come home at all.*

*   *   *

Other letters told about the Fourth of July celebration that year, the new people in the Douglas and Crawford places, how Miss Wilson still asked about Luanna, the long sermons at the church, and Nancy's new blue dress, which she'd never worn because she was saving it for a special occasion. Then Nancy told her how sweet the wild strawberries were, and how she had filled her apron with buttercups from Long Meadow.

When Luanna finally opened her memory box and put the letters inside, she saw the folded paper that Nancy had said not to open until they stopped in Illinois. She took the ribbon off and unfolded it slowly. Lying flat against the paper was a single feather, soft and gray—silver gray, like the tip of a cloud at twilight. It reminded her of the wild passenger pigeons that flew over Midford Falls each spring.

"Oh, Nancy," she whispered. "I haven't changed my mind at all. I've seen things I never dreamed of—I'm not even sorry now that we came—but I still want to come home."

It wasn't until two days later that both Mr. Hamilton and Mr. Douglas discovered that some of their money was missing. "Stolen!" Jeremy Douglas stormed. "And I have a good idea who took it. I caught that good-for-nothing Tyler snooping around my wagons the night before they left us."

He was all set to ride straight after Tyler Crawford, but Luanna's father and Ian managed to get him calmed down. "You can't prove a thing," Luanna's father told him, "and the money's likely all spent by now. Anyway, it was Tawny that was prowling my camp. Looks to me as if father and son were working together."

"Humph," said Mr. Douglas. "If they were, it's the first time they ever cooperated."

The loss of the money made it more important than ever

to get the cabins up and Daniel Hamilton's lathe working. "There's plenty of wood available," he said. "You give me a hand, Jeremy, and we'll turn out as many crates and barrels as we can sell. Might even do some wagon repairs and make some simple furniture. We'll get that money back, and more besides."

The leaves were turning color and dropping in a thick crimson carpet by the time the cabins were up and shelters made for the animals. The living quarters were snug and weather-tight, with the logs hewn smooth on the inside and tight-fitting at the corners. There was even a split-log floor instead of hard-packed dirt, and the fireplace was made of large, smooth stones from the nearby river. But there wasn't any glass in the windows—just sliding doors that kept out the light as well as the cold.

Luanna didn't think the new homes looked like much, and kept thinking about Aunt Prue living in their big frame house in Midford Falls. She stood in the one-room cabin and looked around. "We're going to be crowded," she said, looking at the tiny overhead loft that was to be used for sleeping.

"Probably," her mother answered. "But a good deal warmer than if we stayed outside."

Luanna's father and brothers made a long table and benches, and when the wagons were unpacked and some of their own things placed around the room, Mrs. Hamilton said cheerfully that it seemed just like home. "You know it doesn't," Luanna protested. "It's not like home at all!"

Her mother didn't answer right away. She put the cherrywood clock on the chest against the wall and started it ticking. "It will do just fine," she said finally.

Luanna was so ashamed she took Emmie by the hand, and the two of them went to look for wild blackberries.

When Luanna was watching Emmie, she never had time to think about her troubles because she had to keep her mind on her sister. "She's developed a wandering streak," Luanna told Amy. "I don't dare let her out of my sight."

Two weeks later, when Ben shot a deer, they smoke-dried the meat over the fire, then pounded it into a paste, mixing it with dried currants and some fat. While it was still soft, Luanna and her mother packed it in skin bags and sealed the bags with tallow. "Pemmican like this will last forever," Mrs. Hamilton said. "We'll be glad we bothered, come spring."

But spring seemed far away to Luanna. In October cold weather came suddenly, blowing in from the north and settling down to stay. The house was dark with the windows shut against the chill, and the airless smell of burning candles filled the room. Ben and Eli seemed, with their long legs, to be everywhere. They constantly stomped into the room with muddy boots, and Luanna wished she could smack them with the broom instead of using it on the floor. Nathaniel took to teasing Emmie until she cried, and then he always pulled his innocent face and asked, "What did I do?"

Emmie was constantly underfoot. Luanna had to keep an eye on her and try to do her chores besides. One day, when Emmie was crying because Nathaniel had pinched her, Luanna went outside and closed the door behind her.

She was surprised when it opened a few seconds later and Tink appeared, carrying her wrap. "It's crowded in there," was all he said.

Luanna nodded.

"And noisy," Tink added.

"It's awful, just awful. I hate it!"

Tink was quiet for a minute. "But it sure is cold out here," he told her.

Luanna sighed. As usual, Tink was right. They couldn't stand out there and freeze to death even if it *was* awful inside. She turned and opened the door.

Emmie had stopped crying, and Nathaniel had been put in a chair to sit a spell. He was unnaturally quiet, and Luanna knew her mother must have spoken to him. Ben and Eli had gone into town with Mr. Hamilton. Luanna gave Tink a quick smile and took off her wrap. Then Aunt Clara started in.

"Doesn't do any good to go off in a huff," she muttered. "Why, when I was a girl your age, I did twice the work you do—and never complained about it, either."

Luanna shut her mouth tight. Aunt Clara is after me all the time, she thought. Mother goes on about what a great help she is, but I'm the one who clears the table, washes up, and sweeps the floor.

When Christmas came, Aunt Clara said, "I'm surely glad I didn't stay behind. And I'm mighty glad Prue did." Everyone laughed except Luanna, who heartily wished that Aunt Clara was back in Midford Falls.

She got out the books that Miss Wilson had given her and tried to read a little from Washington Irving's *Sketch Book*. Emmie came and sat close to hear "Rip Van Winkle" and "The Legend of Sleepy Hollow." As Luanna turned the pages, however, the stories took her back to New York's Hudson Valley—not so far from home. She felt homesick and longed to spend Christmas in the house that seemed hers still—even if Aunt Prue *was* living in it. She put the books away and tried writing a letter to Nancy, but that made her feel even worse. Time to take a walk, she thought.

She bundled up and walked out along the frozen banks of the Kaskaskia River. There was beauty in the icy whiteness, and her heart leaped when she saw fresh deer tracks on soft, new snow. She walked as quietly as she could, following the deer's trail. More tracks appeared—boot tracks, this time—and she knew someone was ahead of her. She moved cautiously, wondering who it was. Her brother Ben was a great one for tracking deer, and he had left the cabin earlier. Then again, it might be a stranger. Suddenly the footprints stopped, although the deer tracks continued on. There was one last boot track, then no more. Luanna stood still and looked around. Whoever it was couldn't have disappeared.

A branch brushed against her cheek. She looked up, startled, and saw Ian Douglas perched on a thick limb above her, laughing. He held the branch in his hand and would have tickled her face again, but she grabbed it and gave it a pull. Ian teetered a second before he jumped and landed on both feet.

"Shame on you!" she exclaimed, "trying to scare me like that."

"Oh, Lu, it was too much of a temptation. You had your head down studying the tracks, and you looked so serious . . ."

She was trying to decide whether to laugh or be mad when Ian's expression changed, and he put his hand on her arm. "You don't have to be scared when I'm around —not of anything, Lu."

Suddenly he grinned, scooped up a handful of snow and threw it at her. "Ohhh," she squealed, "just you wait!" She gave him a push that caught him off balance and sent him sprawling. Sheepishly, he climbed to his feet. When he held out his hand, she took it.

"Truce?" he asked.

"Truce." She smiled up into his eyes.

They broke off icicles and sucked them until their lips turned blue, just as they had done growing up in Midford

Falls. Then they walked along the frozen river, listening to the water still gurgling beneath the ice.

After a while Ian took her hand and said, "It's almost like home, isn't it?"

Luanna hesitated a second, then nodded. "Almost," she said.

Sometimes that winter she felt as if she had been through all this before. They were getting ready to go West all over again, just the way they had at Midford Falls. New clothes had to be made and old ones mended. Luanna sat for hours backstitching seams—carefully, for Aunt Clara would inspect every one. Luanna's mother had packed plenty of cloth—the same common, butternut-dyed homespun that Luanna was growing to hate.

"I hate it too," Emmie chimed in, and she carried on until Mrs. Hamilton made her a bonnet out of a scrap of calico. Emmie put it right on and wouldn't take it off.

"She's so taken with that bonnet, she hasn't thought of wandering off for a whole week," Luanna told Amy.

Food had to be prepared for storage. Apples hung in strings from the rafters to dry; salted fish was packed away in a barrel. New supplies of tallow candles and soap were stored away, and the regular supplies of rice, beans, coffee, and sugar were checked and checked again. In January, Luanna had her fifteenth birthday. The spring thaws began in March, and the snow turned to slush and ran in rivulets across the ground. Luanna's father and Jeremy Douglas began watching anxiously for the first blades of grass.

"We need an early start," Mr. Hamilton explained to Ben one night. "We still have to push on to Independence before we can join up with a regular wagon train."

By late April the Hamilton's sheep were shorn, and the wool was traded for flour, cornmeal, chickens, and two fat pigs. They kept the chickens for the eggs, but the pigs ended up ham and bacon. When a trader came up along the river, Aunt Clara got a corncob pipe. It won't last long, Luanna thought, if she doesn't stop lighting it with live coals.

One day, about the first of May, Belvidry Crawford appeared. She was driving their rickety wagon and had the young ones with her. "Pa's dead," she said in a low, flat voice. "He got shot for tryin' to steal a horse."

She got down and stood there in the clearing, not looking one way or the other until Rebecca Hamilton went up and put her arms around her. "Tawny's run off somewhere," Belvidry said, "and I've got these two young ones to take care of. I was wonderin'—it's a long way back to Vermont, and there's nothin' for me there anyhow —would you folks let me come along with you? I can drive my own wagon, but Pa sold most everything we owned, so we don't have any supplies. I—I thought I could work my way—help out, you know . . ." Her voice choked, and she looked at the ground.

Luanna figured this asking for help must be the hardest thing Belvidry had ever done. Amy Douglas was standing beside Luanna, and she said softly, "She's stranded, Lu. Somebody's got to help her."

Martha Tanner was moving quickly across the clearing. "I heard," she said. Her eyes snapped fire, and Luanna could tell she'd like to get her hands on Tyler Crawford, even if he was dead. Tawny, too—not that it would do much good.

"We don't have any family," she said to Luanna's mother. "At least we didn't until now." She turned to Belvidry with a big smile on her face. "You just bring those oxen over by our cabin. My, but they do look half-starved. Isaac and me—we've got plenty of supplies to share, and I'll be glad of whatever help you can give me."

Belvidry stood up as tall as she could with the young ones clutching her skirts. "Much obliged, I'm sure," she said.

So Belvidry was back. After a few days it seemed as if she'd never been gone. She didn't talk about how they'd managed through the winter, and nobody asked. Luanna had to give her credit for one thing. She had a lot of gumption to offer to work her way to California.

Luanna helped her mother with the packing, and watched Emmie, and walked with Ian along the river. Sometimes at night, when she sat with her family by the fire and listened to their voices talking and laughing, the cabin didn't seem as crowded as it had before. She remembered that first night when she and Emmie had crawled into the loft together and Emmie had said, "Snuggle up with me, Lu. I don't feel at home here yet."

But little by little, the four walls had become familiar. Mr. Hamilton had hung a shelf to hold his wife's tea set, and the cherrywood clock ticked steadily all winter long. "I never did see a better fireplace," Rebecca Hamilton often declared, as the big pot bubbled with venison, rabbit, or a chicken or two.

But now they were getting ready to leave familiar things behind. As Luanna packed the dried apples and folded the mended clothing, she thought to herself that she had become two different persons, one of them a girl in common homespun waiting for the signal to "Move Out!" and the other her old self, the Luanna who longed for her home.

Mr. Hamilton picked up their mail for the last time—he brought it in their cabin one afternoon and laid it on the table. Luanna looked eagerly for a letter from Nancy and was surprised when her father stopped her, putting his large hand over hers. "There's been sickness in Midford Falls, Lu. Typhoid fever struck down half the town." She saw him look at her mother, as if for help, and she saw her mother come quickly across the room and take an opened letter from his hand. "Some got better, Lu," he went on, "but there were those who didn't. Nancy was never very strong."

She stared at him, waiting for him to go on. But there wasn't any more. "Luanna, dear . . ." Her mother put her arm around her shoulders.

Luanna shook her head slowly back and forth. "Not Nancy," she whispered. "You must be wrong."

"The letter's from Mr. Addison, Lu. He sent along another letter for you. Nancy wrote it, but never got it posted."

Luanna took the envelope and went quickly outside where she could breathe fresh air. She didn't open the letter until she was far from the clearing, alone at the edge of the river. *Half the town is sick with the fever,* Nancy wrote. *I'll be glad when spring comes, and the grass is green again. Oh, Lu, it isn't the same here without you. I wish we could go back to the way things were.*

Luanna felt as if a door had slammed behind her. There was no way to go back to the way things were! She tried not to think about Nancy. Nancy, buried on Cemetery Hill. She thought instead about the way Nancy had looked the last time she saw her, standing alone on the dusty road. Nancy had given the diary to her and said, "We can read it together—when you come back home."

But now Nancy was gone, and home wouldn't be the same without her. "Oh, Nance," Luanna whispered. "Did you ever get to wear your new blue dress?" The only answer was the sound of the soft spring wind, blowing gently through new leaves. Luanna wiped her eyes before she turned and walked slowly back to the cabin.

Emmie came to meet her. She reached up and took her

hand. "We're going west," she chattered happily. "We're leaving tomorrow for California."

Luanna looked at her and tried to smile. "I know, Emmie," she said. "I know."

Nine

It was still early in May and the grass was barely showing when the wagons pulled out. "Can't wait any longer," Mr. Hamilton said. "It's a good four days to St. Louis, and another two hundred and fifty miles across Missouri before we can join up with a wagon train in Independence."

He helped Luanna's mother onto the wagon seat, and offered to help Emmie up to sit beside her. Emmie hesitated a second, then took Luanna's hand. "I'd rather walk," she said.

Nathaniel and Tink were already herding the sheep and the two milk cows along the path through the woods toward Vandalia. "We'll wait for you in town," Tink called.

Ben took his usual place as driver of the second wagon, but Eli wasn't with him. He said a few quiet words to Mr. Hamilton, then climbed up onto the high seat of Belvidry's rickety wagon and took the reins from Belvidry. Belvidry gave him a startled look and climbed right down. "I—I feel like walkin'," she said.

Eli pulled little Alvin Crawford up to sit beside him. It was the first time Luanna had ever seen Alvin smile.

"Move out!" Jeremy Douglas called.

The oxen strained at their yokes and the wagons lurched forward, creaking in their joints like old people who have been sitting still too long. Luanna stood in the clearing and looked at the three cabins. They were like empty boxes with all the wrappings gone.

She supposed other families would come this way and be glad to find them already made. What would they think when they saw the rough furniture that was left behind? Would they notice the wild violets, planted beside the front door, or the notches that showed how tall Emmie and Nathaniel had grown? Would they walk by the river and see deer tracks in the snow as she and Ian had done?

She turned her back on the clearing and watched the wagons slowly pull away, tilting and swaying as the great wheels sank into holes that were still muddy at the bottom from the spring thaw. She listened as the men cried, "Gee-up! Git a move on there!" Cloven hoofs crunched against the hard-packed earth until the dirt stirred and began to rise, filling the air with a dusty cloud that reminded Luanna to put on her bonnet and tie it under her chin.

Aunt Clara's voice rose, high and shrill. "Luanna!" she called. "Step along there, and bring that child with you!"

Emmie giggled. "She sounds like an old biddy-hen that's laid an egg."

Luanna stared at her sister. "You'd better hush. If she hears you talking like that, you'll be in for it."

"No, I won't. First time she scolds me, I'll run away."

"You silly goose. Where would you go?"

Emmie shrugged. "Somewhere." She looked up at Luanna. "I can get to California by myself."

It was best to ignore some of the things Emmie said.

Once she got an idea in her head there was no shaking it loose. Luanna started along the trail behind the wagons, holding tight to Emmie's hand. "Let's hurry," she urged. "We don't want to walk in the dust all day."

The wagons passed through Vandalia and headed southwest on the trail that would take them the sixty miles to St. Louis. Luanna had to admit it felt good to stretch her legs again. This was a gentle land, with rolling, grassy meadows and low hills covered with forests of oak. Here and there the wild flowers were beginning to bloom, and once a bright red cardinal fluttered overhead.

The trail was dotted with potholes big enough to bathe in, and the wagons often had to veer to one side, making new trails in the soft grass. Everyone who walked kept well out of the way, for there was lots of traffic going west to St. Louis and east to the National Road. By the afternoon of the fourth day, the wagons reached the ferry crossing on the Mississippi River.

"We'll camp on this side tonight," Jeremy Douglas said, "and cross over first thing in the morning."

A lot of other people must have felt the same way, for the evening air was filled with smoke from dozens of campfires. After the supper things were washed and put away, Luanna took her diary a little distance from the camp, sat down on a flat rock, and began to write.

My feet have blisters in new spots. I wonder if my shoes will last all the way to California. I try not to think about home, for there is no going back now, and I don't know what lies ahead. I do know that spring has come and the grass is green again.

She closed the book and opened her memory box. She started to take out Nancy's letters, hesitated, and reached for the stone that she had found that first night on the shores of Lake Champlain. She held it in the palm of one hand and ran her fingers over its smooth shape.

"It's nice, that rock of yours."

Luanna turned around. Belvidry was standing there, looking as if she had come upon Luanna unexpected and didn't hardly know what to do about it.

"I reckon it feels smooth when you rub it like that."

Luanna held out her hand. "You can hold it if you want to."

Belvidry touched the stone gently. Luanna thought she held it like an egg that was likely to break. "Sometimes I wish I was a little rock," Belvidry said. "I'd sit all day long and rest." She fondled the stone, rubbing it with her fingers. "Stones are peaceful things. Not like people. People are always stirrin' things up."

Her face reddened, and she handed the stone to Luanna. "I guess you think I'm tetched."

Luanna didn't know what to say. She guessed Belvidry had had enough happen to her to make her act tetched. She put the stone back in the box.

"I—I heard about Nancy," Belvidry said. "This past winter I kept tellin' myself if we'd stayed behind, my ma wouldn't be dead. But Nancy stayed behind, and the fever took her."

Luanna shut the lid of the box with a sharp click. "A body can go crazy trying to figure some things out," she said. She didn't want to talk about Nancy. Especially not to Belvidry Crawford. She stood up to go, but Belvidry wasn't finished.

"I got somethin' to say to you, Lu. Your ma was awful good to me after . . ." She stopped and swallowed hard. "Anyway, I figure I owe you. It's about Tawny. He's back, Lu. I seen him watchin' you way back there on the road to Vandalia. You'd best keep clear of him."

"But Tawny ran off—you said so yourself."

Belvidry nodded. "Bad pennies have a way of showin' up. That's what my ma always called Tawny—a bad penny."

Luanna looked toward the broad Mississippi River. The sky was almost dark now, and the stars were beginning to shine. The surface of the water seemed to soak up the twilight, as if the river were eager for the day to end. She took a deep breath and let it all out. "Want to walk a ways?" she asked.

Belvidry shrugged. "I suppose it wouldn't hurt none," she said.

They walked along the river bank and then back to the camp. When Belvidry stopped at her own wagon next to the Tanners' she said, "Good night, Lu."

"Good night, Belvidry." There were no other words, but when Luanna thought about it, she figured a whole lot had been said.

In the morning they were up early, urging the oxen into line for the river crossing. The ferries were flatboats with two paddle wheels that turned when a horse on either side walked along a narrow treadmill. They were big enough to hold two wagons at a time—or only one, if it was pulled by three yoke of oxen the way the Hamilton and Douglas wagons were. Luanna watched as a wagon was rolled into place in the center of a ferry, its wheels chained together in case the brakes didn't hold. The treadmill horses started walking, the paddle wheels turned, and the ferry moved slowly out across the broad, brown expanse of water.

When the Hamiltons' turn came, Luanna had to stand up front with the oxen that pulled Aunt Clara's wagon. She could feel the current under her feet—a kind of swooshing motion that made her feel unsteady. It didn't look safe to her at all. The same ferry that had seemed big when it was tied up at the landing now seemed to shrink until it was only a small platform in the middle of the big river, churning a precarious path among steamboats, flat-bottomed skiffs, keelboats, and barges. She was glad when they finally reached the other side and she could put her feet on solid ground.

St. Louis, Missouri, was what her father called a boom town, with the buildings all jammed close to the bluff above the river. At least a dozen steamboats—paddle-wheelers with high chimneys—packed the wharves, and the stores that lined the noisy streets were overflowing with customers. The Old Rock House trading post, the courthouse, and the cathedral looked impressive and had a big-city air about them. But Luanna thought St. Louis was a dirty town.

"I've never seen so many horse flies in my life," she told Amy. "If you don't keep moving, they'll land on you and take a bite." She waved her arms around her face. "I can't stand the things crawling over me. I don't dare take my bonnet off, or they'll settle in my hair."

Amy nodded. "Listen to them buzz—like black swarms of bees. I'll be glad when we leave this town."

It was only a few miles northwest to St. Charles, Missouri, where they took the ferry across the mighty Missouri River. The yellow water was so full of silt, Luanna could see why folks called it the Big Muddy. Uprooted trees that had washed downstream in the high waters of the early spring rains had snagged on the sandbars. They hung now, swaying in the current, waiting to be released when the snow melted in the Rockies in June and sent another great surge of water into the river.

"We struck it lucky," Mr. Hamilton said. "Another month, and we couldn't have crossed at all."

The wagons moved westward again along Boon's Lick Road—the old wilderness path that followed the north bank of the Missouri River and was the main trail west out of St. Charles. "We'll stop at the salt springs near Boonville in a few days and replenish our supply of salt," Jeremy

Douglas said. "I hear there's a regular business there. All those fellows have to do is evaporate the water and put the dry salt in bags. We'll buy direct from them. It'll likely be cheaper."

It took more than a few days, however. Boonville was one hundred and fifty miles from St. Louis, and the road was only a widened trail, jammed with wagons all hurrying to get to the starting-off place at Independence. "We should have left Vandalia sooner," Luanna heard her father say one night. "It's well into May and we're only halfway across Missouri."

"Never mind, Daniel." Mrs. Hamilton reached her arm across his shoulders and rubbed the back of his neck the way she used to back home. "We're all well. That's what matters. And the prairies are beautiful. Another day or two and the wild flowers will be in full bloom."

By the time they crossed back to the south bank of the Missouri at Boonville, where the river twisted away in a wide, northerly curve and left the trail, the wild flowers had raised their heads above the lush grass, and the fields were ablaze with color. "It's like a sunset laid out on the ground," Amy exclaimed. "Oh, Lu, don't you want to walk barefoot in it?"

Emmie heard her, and there was no end to her nagging until they had a wild-flower hunt. "You been promising me, Lu. Every day you say we'll do it tomorrow. I don't want to do it tomorrow. I want to do it today."

Luanna didn't really mind, except that the flowers were so beautiful it seemed a shame to pick them. "You watch you don't go too far," Aunt Clara scolded. As Emmie walked by her, she reached out and caught her by the arm. "Are you hearing me?" she demanded.

"Yes, ma'am." Emmie stared at the ground instead of Aunt Clara. As soon as she could pull her arm loose and get out of hearing she looked up at Luanna and made a face. "I'll show her," she said.

"Don't pay any attention," Luanna advised. "It'll make her happy if she thinks she's spoiled your day."

Amy joined them just as Belvidry passed by, walking along the side of the road with Sally Sue. When the little girl stopped and looked longingly at the fields of flowers, Belvidry reached down and took her hand, pulling her along behind her.

"Luanna," Amy said, "have you noticed how Belvidry doesn't twitch her skirts like she used to?"

Luanna hadn't noticed. "When she knows people are watching," Amy went on, "she stands up real straight. The rest of the time, her shoulders are hunched over." Amy paused. "I feel sorry for her, Lu."

Luanna sighed. "I suppose you want the two of them to come along."

"It won't hurt us none, and it might do them some good." Amy grinned.

They all set off across a hilly field south of the road. As soon as she was knee-deep in prairie grass, Emmie let out a squeal and began to run. Her sunbonnet fell loose and flapped behind her as she reached the crest of the hill and disappeared over the other side. Luanna took her time following. Emmie wouldn't get lost—her legs were too short to carry her very far.

The sun was warm and the air was sweet. Luanna rolled up her sleeves and took off her bonnet, walking slowly up the hill. The blossoms of lavender shooting star hung from the tips of tall, leafless stems. Shiny yellow daisies glimmered among clusters of blue spiderwort, and the soft white blooms of Queen Anne's lace waved gently in the breeze. She stood at the top of the low hill and saw the valley beyond, studded with spreading oaks along a winding stream. Emmie was wandering among the flowers, swishing her arms back and forth over them and singing a little song.

Sally Sue laughed excitedly. "Look, Bel, I found a new one," she cried. Luanna turned and saw them, waist-deep in meadow grass and flowers. Belvidry was walking with her sister, carrying the flowers that she piled in her arms. Amy wandered behind her on the lower stretch of the hill.

Luanna looked back at the wagons. The oxen were plodding along, hardly making any time at all. She could easily walk down to the little valley and be back before anybody noticed she was gone.

"Emmie, wait for me," she called.

Emmie didn't pay any attention. She was filling her skirt with flowers now, walking slowly along, looking for new ones.

Luanna ran down the slope to where the oak trees shaded the stream. The water was clear and cool. She bathed her face and arms, then took off her shoes and waded ankle-deep. Finally, she sat down and leaned against one of the old trees. It was so peaceful. She closed her eyes and listened to the meadow sounds, the gurgling of the water, the birds in the trees above her.

When she opened her eyes, the air felt heavy and damp, and there were clouds overhead. Thunder rolled in the distance like a low, faraway growl. There wasn't another sound except the soft pat-pat of raindrops as they hit the leaves. Luanna scrambled to her feet. "Emmie?" she called. "Emmie, where are you?"

She ran to the top of the hill and stood breathless, looking in all directions while the spring rain gathered force and soaked her hair and clothing. "Emmie!" she shouted. "Emmie!"

The others must have gone back to the wagons. Emmie would be with them. She began to run, across the meadow and along the road. She rounded a curve and saw the wagons far ahead, like dots on the landscape.

The Douglases were bringing up the rear today. Amy was in the back of the end wagon, trying to keep dry. "Where have you been, Lu?" she called. "We thought you got tired and left early. We thought you and Emmie were up front in your wagon."

"Emmie—" Luanna panted. "She came back with you?"

Amy shook her head. "I came back alone after I couldn't find you. Then Belvidry brought her sister back. Oh, Lu, you mean Emmie's—"

Luanna caught her breath and ran. When she reached the Hamilton wagons her mother and father stared at her. "Luanna, what on earth?" her mother asked.

"Emmie—is Emmie here?"

Her mother's face paled. "I thought she was with you."

"She was. That is—she ran down the hill, and I—I thought there was plenty of time—"

Mr. Hamilton spoke then. "Luanna, where are your shoes?"

Luanna looked at her feet, astonished to see them bare. "By the stream," she whispered. "I went wading in the stream."

Luanna had never seen her father move so fast. He handed the reins to her mother and had the men gathered before the wagons were off the road and halted. "You come with us, Lu," her father said. He didn't even wait for her to get on a horse, but started off at a gallop without her. She straddled the big bay that Ben was holding for her and dug her bare heels into his flanks.

The last thing she heard was Aunt Clara muttering about nice girls not riding astride.

Ten

It was raining hard now. Luanna blinked the water out of her eyes and urged her horse across the field where she had walked only a short time before. At the crest of the low hill she reined in and stopped. "Emmie!" she shouted. She twisted in the saddle, straining to see in all directions.

"Which way, Lu?" her father asked. He had ridden for some distance along the crest of the hill and was now reining in beside her.

"She ran over the hill, Pa. She must be in the valley." He looked at her a moment. "Oh, Pa. I didn't see which way she went. She was right there with me picking flowers. She seemed all right, so I sat down and closed my eyes for a minute. I—I must have dozed off."

He glanced at Luanna's bare feet, and she knew what he was thinking. She had let Emmie wander while she waded in the stream. She had closed her eyes and slept while her sister . . .

But how far could a little girl have gone? Luanna looked at the stream winding among the trees, then twisting away until it stretched beyond the next hill and out of sight.

I'll run away, Emmie had said. And when Aunt Clara had caught her by the arm, she had told Lu, *I'll show her.*

The men spread out, some backtracking along the road to Boonville, others heading out across the meadows. "You stay with me," Mr. Hamilton told Luanna, and they rode together down the slope and started along the stream. Luanna stopped to retrieve her shoes. Her bonnet was lying where she had tossed it on the grass. She picked that up too. "Emmie!" she called. "Emmie, where are you?"

There was no answer, only pelting rain and distant hoofbeats. "It'll be dark before long," Mr. Hamilton observed. "Get back on your horse." When she was sitting astride again, his hand reached out and touched her arm. "We'll find her," he said.

They followed the streambed, stopping to shout and listen, then moving on again. "She couldn't have come this far," Luanna insisted.

Her father shook his head. "She could if she had a mind to. The child's strong-willed."

The rain lessened and stopped, the sound of thunder became a faraway muffled rumble. A light wind sprang up and the clouds parted, showing a pale sky. Luanna shivered in her wet clothes. There would be no more sun today. Only twilight, then darkness. "What are we going to do?" she whispered.

Suddenly something moved in the brush beneath the trees. There was a whimpering sound, like a small animal caught in a trap. "Wait, Lu!" Mr. Hamilton warned, but she was already off her horse, running and stumbling, catching her skirts on brambles and branches. She had seen a patch of color and recognized Emmie's calico bonnet. "Emmie," she called. "Oh, Pa, she's here! She's all right!"

"I thought you were Indians come to scalp me," Emmie cried. Luanna scooped her up and held her tight. The whimpering stopped. "You're smothering me," she complained. She stared at Luanna. "I walked a long way, but I didn't get as wet as you did."

"Oh, Emmie." It was all Luanna could say.

Mr. Hamilton looked at the two of them a moment, then walked to a clearing and fired a signal with his rifle. He had a good deal to say to both of them, and Luanna didn't think Emmie was listening until he told her she had to ride in the wagon for a while, whether it made her sick or not.

"Oh, Pa," Emmie complained. But he didn't give in.

By the time the last of the search party returned to the spot where the wagons had pulled off the road, it was dark and time to make camp. There were wet clothes to be dried by the fire that night, and hot drinks to ward off chills. Mr. Hamilton opened the cider brandy and poured some in his coffee. "For medicinal purposes," he said. After Mrs. Hamilton put Emmie to bed, she sat near the fire with her head on her husband's shoulder. "We lost half a day's travel," he told her.

She reached up and touched his cheek. "At least we're all together."

Nobody said another word about what had happened except Aunt Clara. She sat and chewed on her unlit pipe until Luanna came by. "Did you learn something today?" she demanded.

Luanna nodded. She had learned a lot, but she wasn't going to talk to Aunt Clara about it. She waited for a lecture, but it didn't come. Aunt Clara took the pipe out of her mouth and got to her feet. "I'm going to bed," she said. "You can have my place by the fire."

In the morning they started out as usual, except that Emmie rode in the wagon without complaining. Luanna's head hurt, but she didn't say anything about it until the wagons stopped for nooning. By then her throat hurt too, and she felt hot all over.

"No wonder," her mother said. "Galloping around in the rain without so much as a cloak to cover you. I'm not surprised you took a chill."

She boiled some water and made willow bark tea, sweetening it with a little honey. Luanna drank it and tried to eat one of the fried corncakes that had been part of last night's supper.

"You can't walk any more today," her mother told her. "I'll make room for you in the wagon next to Emmie."

"That wagon's full to the brim," Aunt Clara said. "The girl can stretch out on my feather bed."

Aunt Clara had rearranged things so that her feather bed lay on top of three big sacks of flour in the middle of the wagon. The bed wasn't too heavy and could be moved if need be. In the meantime, she said, it gave her a place to lie down.

Luanna felt too sick to argue. She stretched out and closed her eyes. At first it was stuffy in the wagon, and the feather bed smelled of Aunt Clara's strong lye soap. After a while, when the wagons began to roll, a soft spring breeze came in through the front opening and washed over her skin. She slept most of that day and straight through the night, dreaming again and again that she was walking knee-deep in prairie grass, looking for Emmie.

When she awoke the next morning, the fever was gone, but her mother said she wasn't fit to walk. She was to sit with Aunt Clara or ride the big bay. Luanna chose the horse.

It was the first time she had ridden a horse with the wagons, and she was surprised to find out that she got as dirty riding as walking. She was higher up in the dust, that was all. By the end of the day, she was glad to dismount.

There were no new blisters on her feet, but she thought she might be getting some elsewhere. "What are you looking peaked about?" Aunt Clara demanded. "You got to sit down all day, didn't you?"

Luanna tried to ignore her great-aunt, but she always seemed to be right there when she least wanted her, like a pesky mosquito. She was surprised when Aunt Clara handed her the pillow that she usually kept stuffed behind her bony back. "Looks like you need this worse than I do," Aunt Clara sniffed.

Luanna was feeling well again when they reached Independence, Missouri, a week later. She walked with Amy, staying close to the wagons, for the traffic was fearful. They moved along the noisy, crowded riverbank toward a newer encampment at Westport Landing. Traders from Santa Fe, still a part of Mexico, unloaded Mexican silver and gold, piles of soft furs, and thick, uncombed wool. When they were all through trading, these traders loaded up again and headed west with sugar, flour, whiskey, and calico. Indians rode into town on ponies heavy with dried meat and furs. There were mountain men in dirty buffalo skins and Mexicans in bright serapes. A drove of cattle came through, urged onward by loud shouts of "Haw!" and "Git along there!"

The main street was lined with buildings that offered supplies and services to emigrants. It seemed to Luanna that every other place was a blacksmith shop or a saloon. Wedged in between were boardinghouses with big signs in front and shops that displayed everything from bacon and beans to colored beads and hand mirrors. People leaned out of hotel windows and shouted to others in the street below. Wagons creaked and chains rattled. Mules raised their heads and brayed loudly, drowning out the soft lowing sounds of the oxen. Boisterous voices cursed and

laughed, and the stench of animals, dust, and sweat filled
the air.

"I never saw the like," Amy said. She reached over and
nudged Luanna. "Look there. Your Aunt Clara is plumb
speechless."

Aunt Clara peered out from the back end of her wagon,
looking over the rims of her spectacles at the sights. For
once, she didn't have a thing to say. It would be nice,
Luanna thought, if she would stay that way.

"Keep clear!" shouted Jeremy Douglas as a big wagon
with nine pairs of mules tried to pass. The Mexican driver
raised his long whip over his head and gave it a crack that
sent the leather tip all the way along the line. The noise
was terrible, and Luanna was glad Tawny Crawford wasn't
around to get any ideas.

They made camp outside town in a large, flat meadow
where other emigrants like themselves were living in a
kind of tent city. They were waiting for the next train to
be formed. "We're late," Jeremy Douglas said that first
evening. "I hear some big caravans rolled out for Oregon
mid-May." He scratched his chin. "But I reckon smaller
trains make better time, Daniel."

Luanna's father nodded. "But are they as safe?" He
looked around at the tents and wagons that cluttered the
landscape. "Looks like a pretty good crowd to me,
though," he said. "I think we can plan on leaving in a day
or two."

The two of them walked away, still talking, and didn't
come back until Luanna and her mother had fixed dinner.
Then it was nothing but Captain Jeffers this and Captain
Jeffers that, with somebody called Moss Murphy thrown
in now and then like salt in the stew pot.

"There's a train leaving in a few days," Mr. Hamilton
finally announced. "Jeffers is wagonmaster. He's writing up

the resolutions for everybody to sign. We have to agree to help each other, bury the dead, keep the Sabbath, things like that—says we're lucky to have a scout like Moss Murphy. There isn't anything about the trail Murphy doesn't know. He's scouting ahead now, up along the Platte River. He'll join up with us at Fort Kearney, Nebraska." Luanna's father paused for air. "We're late starting, but Jeffers says we'll be all right if we move right along."

That's the way it went for three whole days. Everybody acted breathless. There were last-minute repairs and purchases to be made. Supplies were checked and rechecked. Steel wagon tires needed tightening, and the axles all had to be greased. The women washed and cooked by day and at night they sat around on rocks and wagon tongues and talked about the packing they were going to do in the morning.

Guidebooks were read, discussed, and argued over. "Humph!" Captain Jeffers snorted. "Most of them was written by folks that never stepped a foot past St. Louis. If them fellers followed their own advice, they'd likely be buried on the trail."

"They do read like fiction," Mr. Hamilton admitted. "This one claims the riverbeds are paved with gold! But here's one that has maps . . ."

Captain Jeffers was a big, thick-chested man with a voice like a bull and long, hairy arms that seemed to reach almost to his knees. "I don't take much stock in store-bought maps," he said. "All those wiggly lines don't git you ready for the rough spots." He knelt on one knee and heaped loose dirt on the ground, mounding handfuls to make mountains, smoothing out valleys, and drawing in winding rivers with one finger. "This is more like it," he said.

"I reckon your guidebooks don't tell you that them

sheep you got will chew the prairie grass clean down past the roots," Captain Jeffers warned Mr. Hamilton. He stared at the good merino sheep as if they were ailing. "They ain't much good fer pullin' wagons, are they?"

Luanna's father listened to him for a bit, then went out and sold all but two of the sheep and bought an extra yoke of oxen.

Luanna opened her diary. *I never saw so much excitement and hurry-up*, she wrote.

> *I feel like somebody's chasing me from sunup till dark. When we went into town today for extra supplies, Aunt Clara bought a bag of colored beads and some hand mirrors—to trade with the Indians! Amy and I wanted to watch the medicine show, but Aunt Clara pulled us right along. She said Pa's got better stuff than that in his barrel of cider brandy. Amy and I wonder how she knows so much about it.*

She closed the diary and saw Ian Douglas walking toward her. "Are you ready, Lu?"

"I'm ready to leave this place." She swatted a fly. "The sooner the better."

Ian grinned. "It's the grasshoppers that bother me. They're thick as frogs in a pond, and they jump right up my pants legs. I'll be glad to pull out, all right. Pa says twenty-four families have signed up. They're all well stocked."

Luanna looked across the meadow at the wagons. "They surely are. Most wagons are packed so full the canvas is bulging."

Ian nodded. "Can't be helped. It's two thousand miles to the Pacific, and not many places along the way to get more supplies."

They sat in silence a few moments. "Will we be all right?" Luanna finally asked.

Ian reached out and touched her hand. "Sure we will," he told her. "We've come this far without trouble, haven't we?"

Luanna thought of Nab Crawford lying alone in a grave in the woods. She didn't say anything about it, but she didn't go to sleep until very late that night.

Eleven

"Turn out! Turn out!" Rifle shots sounded with the early morning call. Luanna shivered in the darkness. The roosters hadn't even begun to crow, but there were cows to milk, stock to gather, and breakfast fires to start. Children cried, and dogs barked. The choking dust rose and mixed with wood smoke and the smell of cooking bacon, then settled on the cornmeal mush bubbling in big pots over the fires. By the time breakfast was over and things packed away, the men had yoked the oxen and hitched them to the wagons.

"Hurry along," urged Captain Jeffers. His voice rose above the noise and confusion as he strode through the encampment, ordering people about. "Line up, there!"

They had drawn numbers yesterday, and there was to be no arguing. They would travel in a single row of thirty wagons and pull into a circle at night. Every morning, the lead wagon from the day before would wait at one side and bring up the rear.

At seven o'clock, Mr. Henshaw, a fellow emigrant who still carried his bugle from cavalry days, blew a loud blast, and Captain Jeffers shouted, "Move out!" Whips cracked as drivers urged their oxen forward and tried to find their places in the staggering line. A few mules bolted and ran free. When they were caught, they balked and wouldn't budge—just raised their heads and hee-hawed.

We'll never get to California at this rate, Luanna thought. She looked for Amy and saw her up near the front. The Hamiltons were placed about midway, behind the run-down outfit that Eli had tried to repair for Belvidry and in front of some folks called Bellows, who had come up from Tennessee.

Philander Bellows was so skinny his pants hung from his suspenders in a loose circle around his middle. "My husband won't stay in one place long enough to put on any weight," his wife Betsy told anyone who would listen. "We had a real nice place back home, and he couldn't wait to leave it." She shaded her eyes and peered at the spreading fields of prairie grass and wild flowers. "Likely full of snakes," she said. "Willy Joe, you see you keep to the path, and don't let anything happen to your little sister. You hear?"

Almost everybody could hear Betsy Bellows when she raised her voice. The only ones who didn't pay attention were her two children, Willy Joe and Dora May. Willy Joe was nine going on ten, and Dora May was Emmie's age. They laughed and yelled like wild things and ran barefoot through the grass. "Follow the leader," Willy Joe screamed. Sally Sue Crawford would have taken out after them, but Belvidry got hold of her and hung on tight.

"There are snakes out there for sure," Belvidry told her sister. "Eli told me he saw two big rattlers yesterday!"

Aunt Clara peered out from the back of her wagon. "I reckon they're long gone. I never knew a snake to stay around a mess of confusion like this."

Luanna bit her tongue to keep from asking how many

snakes Aunt Clara had known. She glanced at Belvidry and knew from the way her mouth was twitching that she was wondering the same thing. It gave her an odd feeling to know she was sharing a thought with Belvidry Crawford.

At last all the wagons were rolling, stretched out in a meandering southwest line more than half a mile long. They left the state of Missouri and said good-bye to the United States as they entered the vast, unorganized country called Nebraska. It was a full two days along the Santa Fe Trail before they came to a junction where a track led off to the right. Somebody had stuck a rough post in the ground and attached a sign that pointed northwest. It read, "Road to Oregon."

That was the way they were going, for the Oregon Trail would be their route until they crossed the Rocky Mountains and branched off on the California Trail. But the sign wasn't the only evidence of people who had passed before them. For the last two days, the road had been lined with graves—solemn reminders of the terrible cholera epidemic that had spread along the Missouri and across the plains only a few years before.

The very next night, Philander Bellows got out his concertina and slipped his hands through the loops at each end of the instrument. "Pa's gonna play his squeeze-bag!" Willy Joe exclaimed, and he quickly found his mouth organ so he could join in. At first, the music was cheerful. People tapped their feet and clapped their hands. But when Mr. Bellows leaned back against his wagon and began to play a soft, sad song, families drew close to each other and sat with remembering looks on their faces.

Luanna put a wrap around her shoulders and walked a short distance away from the camp. When she heard someone coming behind her, she wasn't afraid. She could recognize Ian's quick, sure step anywhere.

"Are you all right, Lu?"

She nodded. "I was thinking about that sign in the road. It's good to know that we are finally at the beginning of the Oregon Trail."

"It's the beginning, all right. All of last year's travel was getting us ready for this."

She looked across the prairie meadows that stretched ahead, the tall grass shifting in the moonlight. "I didn't look back when we left our camp at Westport Landing," she told him, "even if it was the jumping-off place. It doesn't do any good to look back, Ian."

She could feel the warmth of his hand on her shoulder. "Only to see how far we've come," he said.

He pulled her a little closer and they stood together, side by side, looking out across the prairie. When she glanced up at him and smiled, his hand tightened on her shoulder, but all he said was, "I reckon we'd better be getting back to the camp."

When they returned to the wagons, Aunt Clara was waiting. She glared at Ian until he was gone, then turned on Luanna. "Doesn't look right," she snapped, "you and that Douglas boy walking off alone that way."

"We only walked a little ways," Luanna said. "Everybody could see us plain as day."

"I saw," muttered Aunt Clara. "Guess I know how a young man acts when he's sparking a girl."

Luanna turned her back and walked away, but she could hear her mother's voice. "Luanna's fifteen, Clara, and Ian Douglas is a good deal older. It's only natural that they should notice each other."

Aunt Clara's "Humpf!" followed Luanna around the side of the wagon, where she bumped headlong into Belvidry.

"I was comin' to talk to your ma," Belvidry said. "I

couldn't help hearin'.'" Her mouth began to twitch the way it had that morning. "Wonder what your Aunt Clara thinks of Eli drivin' my wagon."

"She's an old biddy!"

Belvidry nodded. "That she is." Then she grinned. "But she's got spunk. I reckon she'll make it all the way to Californy." She looked around at the circle of wagons where families were getting ready to bed down for the night. "There's others that won't," she said.

Which ones? Luanna asked later, when she sat by the dwindling fire and wrote in her diary.

> *It gives me an awful feeling to look around at all these people and think back on the lonely graves we saw today. Pa was quiet at the evening meal tonight. He kept looking at one of us and then another. Going to California is turning out to be a lot different than it seemed back in Midford Falls.*

But when she pulled the blanket up over her head against the chill of the prairie night, she thought only of Ian's hand on her shoulder and the gentle way he spoke to her. There was nothing wrong in that, no matter what Aunt Clara said.

The wagons rolled northwest, crossing the swollen Kansas River and camping in the bottomlands near streams. Some spring storms came, with lightning flashes that sliced the sky and thunder that made Emmie put her hands over her ears and cry. But many of the days were fine and warm, and there was plenty of shade from oak, cottonwood, and sweet walnut trees. Early in the mornings, the silvery leaves of the buffalo berry sparkled with dew, and the meadowlarks sang. The sunsets made pink and golden streaks in the western sky. "I wonder if I've died and gone to heaven," Amy Douglas said, while Emmie gathered buttercups that grew near the trail and fastened them behind the oxen's ears.

There were Kanza Indians about, but they mostly studied the intruders from behind the trees. "They won't bother a big caravan," Captain Jeffers said, "but they'll steal a single wagon blind."

As if to prove him right, a wagonload of Irish settlers came rolling down the trail, heading back toward Independence. "Those savages took everything we had," they complained. "We're lucky to have the clothes on our backs."

Willy Joe Bellows celebrated springtime by refusing to walk with his sister any longer. When they stopped for nooning one day, he climbed up on the big mule that had come with them from Tennessee. "Come on," begged Dora May. "Let me up there with you."

"You quit botherin' me. I'm too old to play with girls." Willy Joe tucked one of his father's guns into his belt.

"I'll tell," Dora May threatened. "Pa said next time he caught you foolin' with that gun, he'd whip you good."

"He'll have somethin' else to say when I bring back a buffalo for supper." Willie Joe dug his heels into the mule and rode off across the fields.

His mother watched him ride clear out of sight before she stopped talking to a neighbor about the nice little place they had back home. "Where's Willy Joe going?" she asked Dora May.

The little girl put her hands on her hips. "I been tryin' to tell you, Ma. He took Pa's gun to shoot some buffalo."

"Philander! Philander!" The woman began to scream for her husband. "Willy Joe's gone—rode off on the mule to shoot a buffalo."

Mr. Bellows shook his head. "That boy's been talkin'

foolish ever since we left Tennessee." He glanced uneasily at the sky. "I'll have to go fetch him."

Though it was only noontime, the sky had grown dark. The little white puff clouds that had floated lazily on the horizon now looked black and threatening overhead. As the air cooled and brushed Luanna's skin, thunder sounded in the distance, growling like one of the prairie wolves that watched the campfires from a distance at night.

Mr. Bellows rode off in search of Willie Joe when the rain started. Big splashy drops at first, then the sky opened, and sheets of water flooded the trail and soaked through the canvas tops of the wagons. The lightning hissed and crackled, slicing with a terrible splintering sound through a big oak tree nearby. Emmie screamed and clung to Luanna. "It was close," Mr. Hamilton admitted. "Sounded like the sky was splitting open."

Yellow flames licked up the sides of the tree, and into the branches. But the rain was too much, and the fire quickly sizzled and went out.

Everybody ran for cover. Those who couldn't get inside the wagons got under them, for the hail that had started with a soft, clicking sound was coming down in chunks as big as hen's eggs.

The oxen had been unhitched for the nooning, but not unyoked. Now they lumbered in pairs across the fields, their eyes wide with fright. "Whoa there! Steady now!" It was all the men could do to control the animals and some of the mules simply bolted and ran.

The rain was over in a few minutes, but the wind was still fierce.

"Look there!" shouted Nathaniel. A black cloud whirled and twisted in the distance, forming a giant funnel that raced across the ground, gathering strength as it dipped and swayed and destroyed whatever lay in its path. For a time it seemed to be coming toward the wagons, then it shifted direction and moved away just as suddenly as it had appeared.

"That twister could have finished us," Jeremy Douglas said.

Luanna thought the rain had come pretty close to finishing them. Every single person was soaked to the skin, and most were covered with mud. While the women checked the contents of the wagons for water damage, the men sloshed through the fields rounding up the animals. "We'll be here the rest of the day," Captain Jeffers announced. "Might as well make camp."

Tents were pitched on high ground and firewood was gathered and set out in the sun to dry. The women hung wet clothes on ropes stretched between the wagons. By sunset, most of the animals had been found, and the smell of coffee, bacon, and fried corn cakes filled the air. Aunt Clara killed a chicken that had quit laying, and Luanna's mother put it in the stew pot along with some rice and onions. Ben came by and sniffed appreciatively. "I'm so hungry, my stomach's tucked up under my ribs," he said.

He gave Luanna's hair a playful tweak, then glanced over at the Bellows wagon. "Any news of Mr. Bellows and Willy Joe?"

Mrs. Hamilton shook her head. "Not since they rode out before the storm."

It was almost dark when Philander Bellows came riding into camp on his horse. There was no sign of the mule, but Willy Joe rode up front, held tightly in his father's arms.

"It's about time—" Mrs. Bellows began, but she stopped and stared as her husband swung his leg over the saddle and slid to the ground. Willy Joe's head wobbled loosely, as if it wasn't connected right. His eyes were closed, and his face was the color of chalk dust. Mrs. Bellows came closer. She looked at her husband as if waiting for him to tell her everything was all right. But Mr. Bellows didn't say a word. From the look on his face, Luanna didn't think he could.

"Willy Joe?" Mrs. Bellows tried to take the boy from her husband. "Willy Joe, honey—?"

She stepped back and looked at her hands. They were red. As red as the front of her husband's shirt. As red as the blood that had seeped from Willy Joe and thickened in a dark mass all over his clothes.

Luanna saw her mother move quickly to Mrs. Bellows and put her arms around her shoulders. But it was Mr. Douglas who caught her as she fell. They carried her to her wagon, and still Philander Bellows hadn't moved.

"He shot hisself," he said, not talking to anybody, but saying the words as if they were crowding his mouth and had to come out. "Danged mule fell and broke a leg. Gun went off." He shook his head slowly back and forth. "My boy bled to death. I held him tight, but I couldn't stop the blood from running."

Dora May pushed her way through the crowd of people and stood by her father. "What's the matter with Willy Joe?" she asked.

Nobody answered her. Luanna was surprised when Aunt Clara came forward, took the child by the hand, and led her back to her wagon. The next morning, Willy Joe was buried near the banks of the Big Blue River. "Why are they puttin' my brother in that box?" Dora May demanded. Her blue eyes filled with tears and she pulled on her mother's skirt. "Don't let them close the lid on Willy Joe," she begged. "He don't like it in the dark."

After the funeral, Philander Bellows packed up and turned his wagon around. "We're headin' home," he told Captain Jeffers. "We had a nice little place back in Tennessee. Don't know why we ever left it." He stood a minute, gazing out across the fields of grass toward the western horizon. "It's a long road," he said, "and a mighty crooked one. I hope you all make it."

That night, when they were all sitting around the fire, Eli said, "It was the kind of accident that could have happened anywhere."

But it didn't happen anywhere, Luanna thought. It happened here, on the prairies—where the wild flowers grow.

Twelve

There was little time for mourning on the trail. Early the next morning they pulled out as usual, sending a small party ahead to find a shallow place to ford the Big Blue River. Luanna stopped before they left to put a handful of flowers on Willy Joe's grave. "To show folks we cared," she murmured.

Belvidry Crawford stood beside her, holding Sally Sue by the hand. "We cared," she said. "But we daren't think too long on the bad things that can happen." She squeezed her sister's hand. "Run along now," she told her. But Belvidry's eyes followed her as she skipped along the side of the trail. "I try not to worry about what's coming," Belvidry confided. "Takin' care of today is all I can handle."

When they angled over to the Little Blue late in the afternoon, they were greeted by a small group of travelers who had come west before them from St. Joseph, Missouri, and from Fort Leavenworth, just west of the Missouri River. They had stopped early to repair a broken axle on one of the wagons.

"Halloo there!" shouted a big, red-faced man. "Welcome to our camp. You folks are just what we've been hoping for."

There were four families in all, with only a wagon apiece, but they sounded like an army as they shouted hurrahs at the sight of the larger train. A skinny little man with sharp features pushed himself forward so he could speak up first. He hooked his thumbs in his belt and looked around to make sure folks were listening. "We've been fearing Indians," he said. "Ran into some savages back at Wolf Creek, west of St. Joe. Made us pay tolls to cross the water."

"They were mighty enterprising, those Pawnees." The red-faced man grinned as he stepped forward and shook Captain Jeffer's hand. "Amos Dumfry's the name." He nodded toward the wagon. "My wife, Pearl." Pearl Dumfry tilted her head. She had rosy cheeks and laugh lines around her eyes, and there was a bulge around her middle that made it clear there would soon be another Dumfry in the family. "We're missionaries," Mr. Dumfry explained. "Come all the way from New York and heading for Oregon. Those Injuns didn't give us any trouble, but we're mighty glad we met up with you folks just the same." He smiled at Captain Jeffers and pumped his hand again. "This is fine country. Yes, sir!"

The skinny man pulled out a handkerchief and mopped his face. He introduced himself as Justin Hubbard; his wife was Eunice. Eunice Hubbard looked around and sniffed. She was neat as a pin and wore a short cape with pretty blue forget-me-not flowers embroidered on it, but her lips were all pinched up as if she had a mouthful of vinegar. Luanna thought she looked like the kind of person who'd borrow flour before she'd open her own sack. Justin announced that he was a schoolteacher. "I aim to hold classes noonings and evenings the length of this trip," he said after he'd surveyed the number of available students.

Amy leaned close to Luanna. "I'll bet he doesn't do it for free," she whispered. Luanna nodded. She had heard groans from Tink and Nathaniel and didn't blame them a bit. Justin Hubbard looked like the kind of teacher who liked to use the cane.

A tall young man with fair hair came up to Captain Jeffers and held out his hand. His name was David Thomas. He had a wife and baby, but he didn't seem much older than Luanna's brother Ben. His wife, Sarah, was pretty but shy. She stood close to her wagon hugging their baby boy, who was born on the trail from Ohio. "We're heading for the gold fields," David said, and his eyes sparkled at the thought.

"Gold fever, that's what you've got," roared a short, stocky man with graying hair. He had a wooden leg and a voice that carried clear across the river. His name was Joseph Crane, but everybody called him Doc. He smiled broadly, and thumped David Thomas on the back. Doc Crane makes a lot of noise, Luanna thought, but what she noticed about him most were his hands. They looked strong and rough, but had long, slender fingers that moved when he spoke as if he couldn't talk without them. His wife, Mariah, was a quiet, dark-haired woman with a soft smile.

"And this is our helper," Doc Crane announced, motioning to a young man standing near the wagon. "He buried his poor ma and pa on the trail in Illinois and hired on with some cattlemen as far as St. Joe. I was right glad to find a fellow that's not afraid of work. Reckon he'll finish the trip with us."

Luanna heard Belvidry gasp as Tawny Crawford turned around and took off his hat. He was taller and a little heavier than last year, and his hair had grown so that it hung long around his neck. He wore a gun in a holster slung low on one hip, and when he walked, he swaggered, the way men do when they come out of saloons and look around to see who's watching. Grinning, he walked over to the Crawford wagon.

"Hello, Lu," he said as he passed by. "Still collectin' things for your little box?"

He didn't wait for an answer, just laughed and walked over to Belvidry. "You've growed up some," he told her. "Got Eli Hamilton to do your drivin', I see." He put his hand on her shoulder and spoke in a lower voice. "We have things to talk about, Bel. I intend to have what's mine."

Belvidry pulled away from him and went to where Eli had pulled her wagon into the camping circle for the night. Tawny gave a low laugh. "As if I didn't know where to find you," he chuckled.

He had hardly turned around when Doc Crane stopped him. "What's this?" Doc Crane demanded. "How'd you get to know these people?"

"On the trail," Tawny answered, as smooth as could be. "My ma and pa traveled with them for a bit way back along the National Road. Sure is funny that I should come across 'em this way."

Captain Jeffers said all four wagons could join the train, but they would have to take their places at the end of the line. Nobody complained. It was pleasant the next few days traveling up the twisting course of the Little Blue —plenty of green grass for the stock and lots of shade by the river. The June evenings lengthened into long twilights when there was music and dancing in the circle of the wagons. Doc Crane got out his fiddle and played until the stars came out and the moon was high.

Justin Hubbard's classes weren't much of a success. At

noonings the children waded in the streams and played games in the shade, and they hid when they saw him coming. In the evenings, there were cows to be milked and water to carry from the river. Mr. Hubbard cornered Nathaniel one afternoon and got him by the collar. "Do you want to grow up ignorant?" he demanded.

Nathaniel stared at him. "I'm not ignorant," he said. "My sister taught us our lessons all last winter in Illinois." He wiggled until he pulled loose. "You better let me go, mister. My pa sent me to collect firewood. He says we won't eat supper tonight if I don't hurry up."

Luanna knew that the fire was built and supper was already cooking. Nathaniel knew it, too. "You shouldn't tell a fib," she told him half-heartedly.

That night, alone at the Hamilton campfire, Luanna took out her diary. Tawny Crawford stood to one side watching her, but Luanna thought it best to ignore him. He held a whip coiled in one hand, and his fingers flexed around it restlessly as if he wished he had something to snap at. She wondered if he had forgotten the time she'd tossed a bottle of ink at him.

"I'll walk you to the river," he said finally. He moved closer to her and took hold of her arm with a grip she couldn't shake loose.

People were talking and laughing around the other campfires, and Luanna's mother and father were nowhere to be seen. A trail of children rushed by playing Follow the Leader, shrieking excitedly. Luanna could hear Doc Crane's fiddle and realized the singing would start—everyone would be at the Crane wagon—with nobody watching Tawny Crawford.

"I'm not going to the river with you," she said firmly. "Let loose of my arm, Tawny."

His eyes narrowed. "You Hamiltons always did think you were better'n most people. You're not in Midford Falls now, Lu. All that book learnin' don't count for much when you live in a wagon like everybody else."

He gave her arm a jerk. "You look at me. I like people to look at me when I talk."

She deliberately looked away. "The sight of you makes me sick!"

He gave her a push that sent her stumbling backwards against the side of the wagon. "I'll show you what I do to—"

"No, you won't, Tawny." Ian stepped from behind the Hamiltons' wagon. "You won't be showing her anything." He reached for Luanna and pulled her behind him. His voice was low and even, but there was a steely edge to it that Luanna had never heard before. "I'm telling you one time, Tawny. Put your hands on Lu again, and you'll answer to me."

Tawny stood there a minute, flexing his fingers around the coil of his whip. "But you can put your hands on her whenever you want. Isn't that so? Let me tell you somethin'. Tawny Crawford doesn't scare easy. I'll have my way. You wait and see." He looked at Luanna. "It's a long ways yet to Californy," he told her. Then he turned and walked beyond the wagon circle toward the cottonwood trees that lined the river.

"You all right, Lu?" Ian turned to her. "Why, you're shaking all over." He pulled her close to him.

"I'm just mad, that's all." But she stayed in the circle of his arms an extra second, feeling the roughness of his shirt against her face, wondering what would have happened if he hadn't come.

"How'd you know I was in trouble?" she asked.

Ian smiled down at her. "Your Aunt Clara came running. Said she saw Tawny skulking around. All your menfolk are down talking to Captain Jeffers, and I guess she figured I was next best."

Luanna noticed Aunt Clara sitting over in front of the Douglas campfire smoking her pipe. She looked half-asleep, but Luanna knew better. "I think she has eyes in the back of her head," she told Ian.

He grinned. "She's something special, all right."

Long after Luanna pulled the covers up that night, she lay thinking about what had happened—about Ian and Aunt Clara and Tawny. Aunt Clara was a lot of things, she told herself, but *special*? Who would have thought it?

Thirteen

When they reached the Platte River, Luanna marked the date in her diary.

> *June 20th, 1852: Folks are wondering why they haven't spotted a single buffalo yet. Captain Jeffers calls this the Coast of Nebraska, but there is no seashore here—only bluffs lining a wide, grassy valley with a slow, muddy river coming down the middle. The water is a mile or more wide, but only a few inches deep and full of quicksand. We stood on a sandy hill and saw paths the buffalo follow to the river. The only trees are some cottonwoods and willows on the river's islands. It is a strange and lonely country. In a few days we will begin to follow the river upstream.*

Moss Murphy, the scout that Captain Jeffers had told them about earlier, was waiting for them at Fort Kearney, an army post on the Platte River.

"I declare, Daniel," Luanna's mother sighed. "That man is a sight."

Mr. Hamilton laughed. "You may never see another like him, Becky. He was a trapper and fur trader in these parts many years before he turned guide. Captain Jeffers says he's one of the best trail pilots there is."

"Maybe so," Amy whispered to Luanna, "but when you get up close, he smells real bad."

Moss Murphy did have a peculiar odor about him— a wet-tobacco, sweaty-skin smell that mingled with the stench of dirty buckskins and bear grease.

"It makes a body want to take two steps back when you meet him face to face," said Eli, summing things up in his usual manner. But the man's odor didn't bother Captain Jeffers at all. He threw his arms around Moss as if he'd found a lost brother. After the two of them had hollered and thumped each other on the back, Moss turned to one side and spat a bit of tobacco juice, just missing Nathaniel, who was standing as close as he dared.

Luanna thought Moss had a face like a washed-out gulley, and there was dust settled into every crease. He wore an old hat with the rim turned up in front, Indian-style moccasins, and leggings instead of boots. The knife in his belt had a handle made from a buffalo horn, and a breech-loading rifle hung from his saddle ring. Before nightfall, Moss Murphy had become a living legend in the camp.

"His hair turned white overnight after a grizzly bit off his ear," Nathaniel informed them.

"And he can walk through a forest of sticks and dried leaves, without making a sound," Tink added.

"See that scar on his left hand?" Ben pointed out. "He got that when he was snake-bit and poured gunpowder in the wound. Set it off himself and watched it burn."

Belvidry looked at Moss Murphy a long time before she gave her opinion. "He has restless eyes," she told Luanna. "Quick and restless. I reckon he don't miss a trick."

Captain Jeffers announced they would stop at the fort three days to shoe some of the animals and make any necessary repairs. There was a government post office for those who wanted to send letters. Emigrants could buy provisions from the sutler, a trader who followed the army and brought fresh supplies. There were even fresh eggs and milk to be had. But Luanna thought Fort Kearney was a dreary, dusty place. The tiny four-room hospital inside the walls and the unmarked graves covering the sandy hills served as reminders of the deadly cholera that stalked the trail.

She was glad when the three days were over and they could start along the Platte River that stretched toward them from the high plains. They kept to the south bank, traveling upward through the flat, sandy valley where dry, brown grass stretched away to the yellow sandstone bluffs. But as soon as Fort Kearney was out of sight, she remembered something Moss Murphy had said. There were Pawnees to the north of them and Cheyennes to the south—and it was a long way to Fort Laramie, westward along the Platte.

The air was hot and dry, and Luanna was thirsty all the time. It wasn't long before her lips felt parched, and when she looked in Aunt Clara's hand mirror at the end of the day, she saw that her skin was caked with dirt. "I'm going to look just like Moss Murphy," she moaned.

Amy laughed. "Nobody looks like Moss Murphy."

Three days after they'd left the fort, buffalo were sighted, cresting the bluffs like a dark swarm of bees. The wagons pulled up—there would be no more traveling this day. "There must be thousands!" Ben shouted. He was already on his horse, Ian beside him. Tawny Crawford fingered his whip, and when the other men rode out, he was with them, bringing up the rear.

The animals were coming toward the river for water and grass, but they were well away from the wagons. They were great clumsy-looking creatures with humped backs and shaggy heads, their hides all ragged from shedding their winter coats. But they ran like the wind when they were being chased, and the ground seemed to tremble beneath their weight. Some bulls were killed, and their meat, when it was cooked that night, was dry and hard to swallow.

Mr. Hamilton cut thick steaks, and Luanna helped her mother cook them over the fire. "Smells fine!" Ben exclaimed, rubbing his stomach. He put a big piece in his mouth and chewed it awhile. Luanna watched him, wondering when he would give up and take it out. But Ben wasn't a quitter. He swallowed hard and took a deep breath. "If that stuff was chewin' tobacco, it'd last a feller a lifetime," he declared.

"You got good eatin' there," Moss Murphy said. But Luanna thought the dark meat was tough and strong-tasting. The next day, Mrs. Hamilton and some of the other women cut it up and baked it with dried apples in a pie. It's a strange kind of mincemeat, Luanna thought, but this is a strange country.

Every day was the same. Dawn came quickly in the valley of the Platte. The sun rose as if it meant business, transforming the brown, silty water into a silver sheet, drying the river mists and warming the earth. People came out of their tents and wagons, rubbing sleepy eyes. Cows were milked, breakfast fires were started, oxen were yoked. Captain Jeffers raised his arm and swung it forward, pointing west. "Move out!" he cried, and another day had begun.

When the wagons pulled out, there were scraps left behind as evidence that they had stopped there. Then the wind moved over the spot, covering the wagon tracks with sand, and the plains were silent again. *It's as though we had never been*, Luanna wrote in her diary. *There's hardly a sigh for remembrance.*

Moss Murphy went ahead every day and found a spot for the night, marking out the circle so that the wagons pulled into place with surprising accuracy. Cows were milked again and dinner fires were started. Water was carried from the river, and buffalo chips—flat, dried pieces of dung—were gathered for the next morning. By eight o'clock, the evening meal was over. The first watch was set, and the guard was on duty. Doc Crane got out his fiddle and played for a while. Then the camp grew quiet, resting until the sun came up, and they could start all over again.

Ever since Amos Dumfry had joined the train, Sunday was called a day of rest, though Luanna didn't see that folks got much of it.

Mr. Dumfry would get out his Bible and read the same passage aloud:

> The Lord thy God bringeth thee into a good land, a land of brooks of water, of fountains and depths that spring out of valleys and hills; a land of wheat, and barley, and vines, and fig trees, and pomegranates; a land of oil olive and honey; a land wherein thou shalt eat bread without scarceness, thou shalt not lack any thing in it . . . thou shalt bless the Lord thy God for the good land which he hath given thee.— Deuteronomy 8:7-10

"It is a hopeful thought," Luanna's mother said. "We'll keep it in mind while we do the washing."

Luanna hung the dripping clothes from ropes tied between the wagons and hoped they'd dry before the dust could settle on them and turn to mud. She did not want to have to wash them over again. There was still bread to be baked, and the remaining buffalo meat had to be cut into thin strips and dried in the sun.

Everyone worked in the camp. The men put grease on the sore hoofs of the animals. Sometimes they added precious gunpowder to help cauterize open sores. They repaired the wagons, and hunted more buffalo. Children were sent out to pick berries and gather buffalo chips. When they had free time, they looked for the prairie dogs. These funny little animals would inch out of their holes early in the morning and stand sniffing the air awhile before they'd decide to stay on top for the day.

Luanna thought it was awful to spend her days picking up buffalo dung, but she got used to it—there wasn't anything else to burn for fuel. And there were advantages. The flat, sun-dried chips did make a hot, almost smokeless fire, and Luanna heard Moss Murphy tell her father that "a piece of buffalo meat cooked over dung don't need no pepper."

She and Emmie filled their aprons, then dumped their chips in the sling that Mr. Hamilton made and attached to the wagon. It took three whole bushels to make a fire big enough to cook a meal. The boys had to dig trenches to keep the chips from blowing away in the wind.

"I feel like I want to wash my hands all the time," Luanna told Belvidry.

"Won't do no good," Belvidry told her. "The only time we're not handlin' chips is when we go to bed at night."

Luanna learned to clean the cooking pots with sand from the river, to bury a covered pot of beans in hot embers overnight, to keep the firestones hot so the water would boil quickly in the morning, and to carry a stick when walking, for rattlesnakes were plentiful. The snakes blended in so well with the tall, dry grass that it was easy to come upon one without seeing it.

They had been on the trail about a week since Fort Kearney—three days out from the fork of the Platte where the river divided—when the wagons stopped for a few hours to wait for Pearl Dumfry to have her baby. It was a little girl with blue eyes, and Amos said they would name her Adamina, which meant daughter of the earth.

"It's a good sign," Aunt Clara said, but Eunice Hubbard pinched her mouth up tight and muttered, "One more mouth to feed."

The very next evening, a skunk wandered into camp and rummaged around in the Hubbards' wagon. When Eunice saw it, she screamed and the skunk raised its tail. Justin Hubbard had to pull to the end of the line and stay there a few days.

"I guess Eunice won't be doing her sniffing for a bit," Aunt Clara said. "Takes a long time for skunk to wear off." Luanna thought she'd never seen Aunt Clara look so pleased.

The following morning, however, nobody was smiling. A large number of Cheyennes had put up their tepees on the flatlands near the river. "Lookin' for buffalo, I reckon," said Captain Jeffers.

Moss Murphy nodded. "Until they seen us, they was." He passed the word. All the men were to carry loaded rifles as the train passed by the Indian camp. It was important not to look afraid. It was also important not to get trigger-happy.

"I'd as soon shoot an Injun as a buffalo," Tawny Crawford muttered. "It's no more'n target practice." But he shut his mouth when Captain Jeffers gave him a warning look.

"You'll answer to me," he snapped. "There was a peace treaty got signed at Fort Laramie last year, and I don't aim to be the one to break it."

Mrs. Hamilton put Emmie in the wagon and made Luanna get inside, too. Tink and Nathaniel boasted that

Injuns didn't scare them one bit, but Mr. Hamilton told them to climb up on the wagon seat with Ben. The train passed the camp without incident—close enough to see the painted designs on the tepees, the children running and playing, and the women stretching buffalo skins to bleach in the sun. Some stopped what they were doing to watch the wagons roll slowly by. I wonder what they think of us? Luanna thought. They seem peaceful enough.

But she felt a prickle go down her spine early the next morning when a band of Cheyenne braves rode into their camp before the breakfast fires had even been started. They were a proud-looking group, sitting gracefully on their horses. They had paint on their faces and wore feathers in their hair. One of them did most of the talking with Moss Murphy. He wore a beaded necklace with long decorations that hung in a semicircle on his chest. Tink sneaked over and had a look. When he came back to the tent, his eyes were wide.

"Real fingers!" he exclaimed. "Those decorations came off somebody's hand."

Luanna swallowed hard, trying not to imagine how they'd got there.

When the Cheyennes had left, Moss Murphy and Captain Jeffers called a general meeting. "They don't want us to go any farther," Moss Murphy announced. "They say we're killin' all their buffalo."

"What about the treaty?" Justin Hubbard wanted to know. "We have a right to pass through this land."

"Injuns got rights, too, and there's more of them than us."

"I say we fight," Justin muttered.

Tawny Crawford moved to stand beside him. "We could clean out that whole Injun camp before suppertime," he said.

Murphy leaned over to spit. "And bury half this wagon

train while we're about it." He looked at Captain Jeffers. "They want us to make a feast. It'll run our supplies short, but I don't see no other way. Otherwise, they aim to keep us here, and they got ways to do it."

In a short time, the fires were hot, and cornmeal mush was bubbling in the pots. "They want bread," Murphy told the women. "You'll have to stir some up."

"Bread takes time," Eunice Hubbard complained.

Moss Murphy took off his hat and scratched his head.

"You've got the rest of your life, ma'am," he told her.

Fourteen

The cooking and bread-making went on all day. When big kettles of the corn mush were set out in a row, the Cheyennes came in masses, singing and dancing. Luanna had never imagined anything like it. They moved with grace, flexing their knees and marking out a repetitive pattern of steps with their feet. Their voices blended in a high, singsong chant.

"I reckon it's their war dance," Nathaniel said.

They did look warlike with their painted faces and feathers, but they didn't seem angry. They drank coffee, hot and black, and when the bread was ready, they broke it into steaming chunks, tossing the pieces in their fingers to keep from being burned.

The singing and dancing went on, even while they ate, and when they finally went back to their camp, it seemed strangely quiet. Dark was coming on, and the men brought the stock inside the circle for the night. The women tried to piece together some supper out of the leftovers.

"They just about stripped us of bread-stuff," Mrs. Hamilton said. "We don't have near enough to take us to Fort Laramie."

Mr. Hamilton came and put his arm around her. "We can eat pemmican, Becky. There's plenty of buffalo, and the boys saw some prairie chickens yesterday. We'll stock up again once we reach Fort Laramie. At least the Indians are letting us alone. We ought to be thankful for that."

But when they yoked the oxen in the morning and started up the river, Luanna looked back and saw the Cheyennes coming along behind. They had taken down their tepees and packed everything on a kind of traveling rack that Captain Jeffers called a travois. It was made by fastening two poles at a horse's shoulders, the ends dragging behind. Saplings were laid between the poles and fastened with thongs, making a frame to hold the bundles.

"It makes my skin crawl to have them comin' up behind me like that," Belvidry said when the train stopped for nooning. "You suppose they're goin' to follow us all the way to Californy?"

Nathaniel shook his head. "They'll likely scalp us first," he told her.

Eli climbed up on the seat of Belvidry's wagon and pulled little Alvin up beside him. "I should've gone to college in Midford Falls," he said.

"You were the one who wanted to see the Pacific Ocean," Luanna reminded him.

When the wagons stopped to make camp for the night, the Cheyennes stopped too, and it wasn't long before they came riding up with beaded moccasins and smelly skins to trade for tobacco, cloth, and more bread. They roamed freely around the camp, examining the wagons, the horses, and the women's cooking pots.

When they left, some things were missing. "Where's my fire shovel?" Eunice Hubbard demanded. "I laid it by the pot, and I don't think it got up and walked away." She turned to her husband. "One of them Injuns took it. If you don't fetch it for me, there'll be no dinner tonight."

Her husband glared at her. "Woman," he said, "if you don't close your mouth, I'm going to saw this wagon through the middle and you can choose your half!"

Mrs. Hubbard was silent, but she came to borrow one of Mrs. Hamilton's shovels that night. "Good thing you had two," Aunt Clara said. "You'll never lay your eyes on that one again."

The Cheyennes followed the train for three days—all the way to the forks of the Platte River and then up the banks of the South Platte. Every evening they came riding into camp to trade, and no one dared refuse them.

Sarah Thomas, who was heading for the California gold fields with her husband David and their baby boy, shook her head in dismay. "I've got a pile of dried buffalo meat that smells like dead flies," she told Luanna. "I wouldn't put the stuff in my mouth if I was starving. I had to give up a sack of beans and a pot of cornmeal mush to get such a toothsome prize."

It was the Fourth of July when Captain Jeffers stopped the wagons at the fording place of the South Platte, but nobody said a word about celebrating. There was a small, makeshift trading post set up on the bank above the river, and Eunice Hubbard made her husband stop so she could buy some flour. When she opened the bag they sold her, however, it was full of weevils. Justin Hubbard would have traded it back for whiskey, but he said the two men who ran the post had drunk up their supply.

The men set to work unloading the wagons and waterproofing them the best they could for the river crossing. Some folks went over to the Cheyenne camp and bargained for extra buffalo hides to fasten over the wagon boxes to keep the water from leaking in. Others finished their waterproofing by stuffing the cracks with pieces of cloth and caulking up the seams with tar.

"We'd best double up on teams," Captain Jeffers advised. "I want to see eight oxen or more pulling every wagon. That means we take turns crossing, then swim the animals back and use them again. We've hit it lucky," he added. "Water level's down, but it's still a long crossing. Protect your supplies as best you can."

"The river looks big as a sea to me," Amy said.

Luanna nodded. "It must be a mile or more wide here. And see how fast the water runs!"

It took all day to get the wagons ready, and there was lots of talk about what could happen on the way across. "I hear the current's bad," said David Thomas. "It can pull a wagon sideways and turn it over."

Sarah Thomas gave a little gasp and held her baby tightly. "I don't know why I let David talk me into this," she told Luanna. "Ohio wasn't half bad. Only thing it didn't have was gold."

"Quicksand's worse than current," Justin Hubbard told them. "Fellow told me he saw it swallow up a whole wagon and pull the team right in behind it. He said those short-legged oxen sank to their bellies before they hardly got wet. That's why I'm driving mules."

Moss Murphy was passing by and heard what Justin Hubbard was telling folks. He scratched his chin and leaned over to spit. "You better watch out for them mules," he said. "Let them critters get water in their ears and they'll kick up their heels and drown ever' time." He looked straight at Justin. "That's the truth," he told him.

Mr. Hubbard didn't have much to say, but soon after Luanna saw him staring at his team with a thoughtful look on his face. A little later he and Eunice were tearing up strips of cotton cloth to stuff in the animals' ears.

The next morning, just before the crossing, a few

Cheyennes wandered into camp. "They must've smelled our mush cooking," Eunice Hubbard grumbled.

Belvidry came up to stand next to Luanna. "Look," she whispered. "It's not mush they're after."

One of the Indians was pointing at Eunice's cape with the blue forget-me-nots on it. He motioned for her to take it off.

"Oh, Justin!" she called out in alarm. Then she saw what the young man was offering for trade. "You've got my fire shovel!" she exclaimed. "You wicked savage!"

Justin Hubbard peered around from his wagon seat. "What's the trouble now?" he demanded.

His wife was fuming. "This filthy thief wants the clothes off my back—the very cape I've worn all the way from home. You better do something, Justin."

Mr. Hubbard nodded. "I aim to. When Captain Jeffers gives the signal, I'm heading for the other side of the river. You coming?"

Eunice Hubbard glared first at her husband, then at the young man. She unbuttoned the cape and handed it over, reaching with her free hand for the shovel. "I'd like to give you a piece of my mind," she snapped. Luanna figured she would have, too, but the wagons began to inch forward, lining up along the river bank, and Mrs. Hubbard wasn't about to be left behind. She clambered up on the seat next to her husband and wouldn't look back.

But Luanna did. She saw several of the Cheyennes taking turns trying on the cape. For a split second they reminded her of her brothers when they were joshing each other and having a good time.

"Look there." Amy pointed toward the Cheyenne camp. "They're packing up again so they can follow us." But the Indians made no move to follow the wagons across the river and it wasn't long before they headed downstream the way they had come.

"I'm not sorry to see them go," Luanna's father said. "We've got enough on our minds today without fretting about them."

Captain Jeffers went through the train giving every family instructions. "There's quicksand in the river for sure. You won't get pulled under, but you could get stuck. Once you're in the water with your wagons you've got to keep moving."

Returning to the front wagon, the captain swung his arm forward and led the way into the swirling water. Everybody rode in the wagons except the men and some of the older boys, who rode on horseback alongside the oxen, urging them on. Wagons rumbled and creaked down the sandy banks and hit the river with a splash. The strong current pulled them quickly sideways, and the yellow water swirled around the great wheels with noisy, slurping sounds. Whips cracked, and the men shouted and cursed as the short-legged oxen staggered in the treacherous sand.

"Haw! Gee! Git along there!"

The lead wagon carrying Pearl Dumfry and her baby girl gave a lurch and tilted to one side. Pearl's voice rose in alarm. "Amos! Oh, Amos!" she screamed.

Amos's voice didn't sound like it came from the man who read scripture every Sunday. "Tarnation!" he roared. "Git on, you blasted animals. I'll have your hides!" The whips cracked again, and the oxen strained forward. Mrs. Hamilton sat next to Ben, holding on tightly. Her face was white, but she never made a sound of fear, even when Emmie let out a shriek.

"The water's coming in!" she cried. "Ohhh . . . I don't like it. I want to get out of here." She clambered over Luanna, trying to pull her skirts up and away from the water. It was rushing through the wagon cracks as if they had never been stuffed and tarred.

"Oh, Mother," Luanna moaned. "It's soaking everything in sight." She reached out and put her arms around Emmie, who was starting to sob.

"We're sinking, Lu," Emmie cried. "I can feel us sinking!

"Hush, Em. My feet are wet too, and my skirt is soaked. It's just a little water—nice and cool on such a hot day."

She tried to keep her voice steady and her hands from shaking as she held Emmie tightly. The water was filling the bottom of the wagon box, swirling around her ankles. She could see out front where the oxen were staggering against the current, struggling through the treacherous sand beneath their feet. The far bank of the South Platte seemed as distant as the horizon.

"Oh, Mother—" Luanna whispered.

The wagon gave a sickening lurch, tilted crazily, and stopped moving. "Blast!" Ben cursed. Luanna had never seen him use the whip before, but he used it now, lashing out at the oxen with a fury that brought them to their feet. Mr. Hamilton moved his horse closer to the oxen's heads. "Hiyee! Yeehaw!" he yelled, and the wagon lurched again and slowly began to move forward.

"Hush, Emmie. Don't cry," Luanna whispered. "Everything's all right now."

Emmie sniffled and reached for a piece of Luanna's skirt to wipe her nose. "I'm not crying," she insisted, "but I will be if you don't stop squeezing me so tight."

Mrs. Hamilton looked over her shoulder and gave Luanna a shaky smile. "We're doing fine," she said. "We'll be across before you know it."

But it took the better part of an hour before they reached dry land. They unhitched and rested the oxen a bit before Mr. Hamilton and Ben could swim them back to pull another wagonload. "It's like a relay race," Emmie said, " 'cept nobody's goin' very fast."

Belvidry's wagon made it across next with Eli driving and Mr. Hamilton and Ben urging the oxen on. When they were on dry land, Eli lifted Sally Sue and Alvin down, then reached up to help Belvidry. Luanna saw how his hands stayed around her waist an extra second before he let her loose. "Much obliged, Eli," was all Belvidry said.

Then came Doc Crane, sitting on the high seat of his wagon with his wife Mariah. Tawny rode in the water, cracking his whip and yelling at the oxen. They got across just fine, but Doc Crane climbed down in a hurry and he looked as mad as a hornet. "You're supposed to crack that whip over the animals' heads," he bellowed at Tawny. "I saw you lay it right on their backsides."

"You got across, didn't you?" Tawny retorted. He turned away, but Luanna heard him mutter, "No one-legged feller tells *me* what to do."

"I'm worried about Aunt Clara," Luanna's mother said. "She wouldn't budge from her place in the back of that wagon. If the quicksand catches them like it did us, she could slide right out." She gave Emmie a stern glance to stop her giggles. "It's not a laughing matter," she said. "It's a good thing I put Tink and Nathaniel in there with her."

When the wagon finally arrived, with Mr. Hamilton leading and Ben driving, Tink and Nathaniel climbed out fast. "Wheeou!" Tink exclaimed. "You should've been there. Aunt Clara knows words I never—"

Nathaniel gave him a poke, and he shut his mouth. Aunt Clara had climbed out by herself and was shaking out her wet skirts as if it was something she did every afternoon. "It's a good thing you sent those boys along with me," she told Luanna's mother. "They never would have made it by themselves."

"You were the one—" Tink began, but Nathaniel poked him again.

Aunt Clara had found a dry match and was lighting up her pipe. "Well," she said, looking back the way she had come, "that's one less river to cross."

Fifteen

That night Amos Dumfry got folks together and said a prayer of thanks. All the wagons had crossed the river safely.

Doc Crane got out his fiddle. "In honor of the Fourth of July," he told his audience. He began to play "Yankee Doodle" and a few tired voices joined in, but no one tried to get up and dance.

"My legs are wobbly," Sarah Thomas said. She leaned against her wagon, holding her baby in her arms. "I feel like fallin' down, I'm that tired."

Luanna wondered what it would be like to be married to someone like David Thomas. With his gold fever, he spent all his evenings talking with the men and hardly ever looked at Sarah. The baby began to fuss, and Sarah put him over her shoulder. "Let me hold him for a bit," Luanna offered.

Sarah looked uncertain. "His breechcloths need changing. I—I should've done it sooner, but . . ."

"Never mind that." Luanna held out her arms. The

baby did smell sour, but not any worse than the way a lot of people smelled lately.

Someone began singing softly, "On the sea, the deep blue sea, gladly, gladly would I be—"

"Not me!" Emmie's voice rang out clearly. "I had enough water for one day." She looked at Aunt Clara to see what she would say to that, but Aunt Clara didn't hear her. She was sound asleep before the fire, her pipe still in her mouth.

The next morning, Luanna's mother tried to salvage some of the wet flour. She stirred it up with more water and made a thick dough that she cut in pieces and fried in hot fat. The result was edible, and the little brown biscuits would keep for days, but Luanna confided to Amy that they tasted like river water.

"I think I'll put one in my memory box," she said.

Amy laughed. "If you ever get real hungry, you can always take it out and eat it."

According to Captain Jeffers, they were more likely to get thirsty. "We have to carry our water for a few days," he said. "Fill up every empty container, and make sure you plug those leaky barrels." He looked at Belvidry's wagon.

"They're the only barrels I've got," she told him, "and I've plugged them till they won't plug no more!"

Eli helped her melt down some tallow and stuff it in the cracks. "It'll hold awhile," he told her, "but the wood's in bad shape."

Belvidry nodded. "So's the wagon, but it's all I've got." She sent him a glance that said she didn't quite mean that. Luanna had seen her mother look at her father the same way when she wanted to let him know she was glad he was nearby.

The wagons moved out, angling away from the river on a steady uphill climb to the high plateau at the top of the bluffs. When they stopped for nooning, the oxen ate the short brown grass, then lifted their heads and bawled for water. The air was hot and dry, and heat waves floated like pale silk, shimmering on the horizon. Luanna tried not to think about how thirsty she was.

By the end of the second day, they reached the edge of the plateau where the trail seemed to end. In reality, it plunged off the side of a cliff into the valley below.

"Plenty of water down there in Ash Hollow," Captain Jeffers promised, "but you'll have to go head-over-heels down Windlass Hill to get to it tonight."

After helping to clean up the dinner things, Luanna walked over to the edge with Ian to take a look. The slope was almost perpendicular. "Why, you could slide down easier than you could walk," she told him.

"That's just what folks are goin' to do in the morning," he said. "You'd best plan on getting a little dusty."

"Look at me now," she laughed. "You know, if there's really water down there, I'm going to jump in with my clothes on."

He smiled at her. "You'll have lots of company." Suddenly he reached out and took her hand. "Are you still sorry you left Midford Falls, Lu?"

His fingers were warm around her own. She looked up and saw the question in his eyes—the one he wasn't asking. "Midford Falls was yesterday," she told him. "It was a good yesterday, wasn't it?"

He nodded, but he continued to look at her, holding her hand, waiting. She took a deep breath. "I'm not the same person I was back there, Ian. I think about different things."

"Such as?" he asked her.

"Well, this might sound strange, but I wonder where the wind goes after we don't hear it anymore. Do you know what I mean? I listen to the wagon wheels and the prairie dogs, and the coyotes crying at night, and the sounds of people when they're happy or sad. I watch the grass bend low in the evening breeze, and I think the world might have been this way when it was young." She shook her head. "I feel dirty, and I'm thirsty."

His arms went around her and felt strong, supportive. She rested her head against his chest for a second before she lifted her face and felt his lips gently touch hers.

"Luanna Hamilton," he whispered, "I reckon we've changed together."

They walked slowly back to the wagons. Aunt Clara was sitting alone by the fire. She looked first at Luanna, then at Ian. "Humph!" was all she said.

In the morning, everything loose inside the wagons was tied down or secured in some other way. The wheels were chained to the wagon boxes to keep them from rolling, and the oxen were hitched up at the back so they could pull against the grade. Extra ropes were attached to the axles. Some of the men would pull on these, and some would be up front at the tongue to help steer.

"Nobody rides," Captain Jeffers ordered. "If a wagon turns over on this slope, it'll end up splinters at the bottom of the hill. I don't want folks breakin' their bones that way."

Women and children climbed down the rocky cliff path the best way they could, sometimes sitting, sometimes sliding, always holding on to each other. Nathaniel and Tink put Aunt Clara between them and tied a rope around her waist. "If the rope was longer, we could let you over the side," Nathaniel teased, and got rapped on the head for his trouble.

Inch by inch, the wagons were lowered. Except for the grating of wheels against rock and the bawling of the oxen, there was hardly a sound. Once folks started down, they seemed to have one idea, and that was to get to the bottom. When they did, and the wagons followed, it was without a single mishap, much to the disappointment of Tink and Nathaniel. They were hoping they'd get to see a wagon fall.

Ash Hollow seemed like Paradise after the hot, dry plains. Numerous streams ran cool and deep. Tall ash trees grew along the banks, spreading their branches and casting wide green shadows on lush meadow grass. Cold, clear water bubbled from a spring, and berries were ripening on the bushes. People and livestock drank their fill, then rested on the cool grass in the shade.

"We'll stay two days," Captain Jeffers announced, and a cheer went up, breaking the strange silence that had followed the wagons down Windlass Hill.

In the middle of a green meadow was a clear pond, fed by a spring. Luanna took off her shoes and walked across the grass, then knelt at the edge of the water and saw herself in the glassy surface. She pulled off her bonnet and looked again. Her forehead had frown marks from squinting in the sun, and her skin was streaked with sweat and dust. She leaned over and washed, watching the water in her cupped hands turn to mud.

"Never mind, Lu," Emmie giggled. "It's just a little dirt. It'll wash right off."

Luanna scooped a double handful and splashed it at her sister. In a minute they were both soaking wet. Their skirts clung to their legs and pulled at them when they tried to walk. "Aunt Clara says she'll slit mine for me," Emmie confided. "She's been nice to me ever since I got lost."

Luanna tugged at her skirts. "That so? Maybe I'll get lost and see if she'll be nice and slit mine, too."

To her surprise, Aunt Clara offered. "You can't walk all the way to California with your skirts hanging in the grass," she said. "Everything you own will be ragged, and the bugs will crawl up your legs."

She cut the skirts up the middle, front and back, and

stitched a seam so that they were like long, loose-legged pants. Luanna gathered the bottoms around her ankles and tied them with twine. It was wonderful not to have to be pulling her skirts free all the time. When Eunice Hubbard turned up her nose and said a thing or two about decency, Aunt Clara silenced her. "You don't see slit skirts blowing up in the wind, do you?"

Luanna wondered how California could be any better than Ash Hollow. Folks rested and mended their wagons, and gathered wild rose hips for tea. Once they'd washed their clothes and themselves, they began to smell a whole lot better. When it was time to go, most people weren't in a big hurry.

"I'd just as soon stay right here," said Sarah Thomas, but her husband looked at her and laughed. "What's a little valley like this got to offer besides shade trees and water?" Sarah climbed up on the wagon seat without a word, but her eyes looked behind her longingly.

"Humph," Aunt Clara said. "It would give me a stomachache to live with the likes of that man."

Luanna nodded. It gave her a strange feeling to be agreeing with Aunt Clara.

The train moved up to the North Fork of the Platte River and followed it along the south bank toward Fort Laramie. "We've got to move right along," Captain Jeffers urged. "You folks act like California's around the next bend."

They were in the high plains now, and the snow-capped peaks of the Laramie Mountains could be seen on the far horizon. The trail climbed steadily along the river. Days were hot and dry, and dust devils whirled in the sand. The sky seemed big and full of sun, and sometimes Luanna wondered if she could take one more step. But at night the heavens seemed to open, the stars shone brightly, and the air was so cold folks wrapped themselves in blankets and shivered. When they finally found a few cottonwood trees growing by the river, they cut them down and built a great wood fire.

There were days when Luanna felt a rhythm as the grass rippled in the wind—as if the earth were sending out pulse-beats from the heart of the land. There were other days when the alkali dust rose so thick that handkerchiefs were held over faces and sweat-soaked clothes soon caked with mud. The wagons rolled on, stopping only for birthing and dying.

Elizabeth Whitcomb, who had joined the train with her husband Jake way back at Westport Landing in Independence, had a baby boy one afternoon soon after they reached the North Fork. "How you feelin'?" Jake asked her.

"Pert enough to travel," she told him, and the wagons pulled out.

Old Solomon Miller, who was going west with his son's family, took sick one night and died before morning. "I reckon it was his heart," his son Matthew said. "It plumb tuckered out."

When Amy Douglas stepped in a hole and twisted her ankle, Jeremy and Ian pulled their wagons over just long enough to bandage it up. But everybody else kept moving along. It was the law of the trail.

One night there was a wedding. Polly Borden and Thomas Kramer decided they couldn't wait till they got to California. "They been eyein' each other since we left Westport Landing," Amy giggled.

Amos Dumfry was in fine form at the ceremony, spouting out bits of wisdom like water from an everlasting fountain.

"You must climb the mountain before you can see the valley," he said. "When night falls, a new day is rising." But when he had a little cider brandy and started in on

" 'Tis better to lose the anchor than the whole ship," his wife told him it was time to go to bed.

Everybody drank coffee now, even the children, because the water tasted so bad. They browned the green coffee beans in a skillet, and the pungent flavor helped hide the strong taste of alkali in the drinking water. Justin Hubbard claimed he even gave a drink of coffee to his mules.

They passed through Sioux country along the North Platte, but didn't see any Sioux. There were buffalo by the thousands, and occasionally they came right up to the camp and sniffed at the oxen. "Get away!" Aunt Clara fumed, flapping her apron at a big bull. He looked at her curiously, then turned and wandered off.

Luanna learned to dig wild turnips and bake them in hot ashes. There was no butter, for the cows had quit giving milk, but her mother showed her how to split the turnips open and add a little bacon fat. Sometimes she crumbled dried sage in her fingers until it was strong and sweet, then added it to the stew pot. "It makes prairie chicken taste real good," her father commented.

When Amos Hubbard spotted Courthouse Rock, sitting like a great cream-colored castle on the plains, and the two square towers of Jail Rock nearby, he stood in silence and took off his hat. These landmarks meant they were less than a week's travel from Fort Laramie. But most folks were more interested in the post office sign that was scratched into the side of the sandstone cliff. Luanna had heard that it was a common practice along the trail for folks to use this spot as a depository for letters to friends or family who were coming later. She watched as Captain Jeffers took a pile of papers from a dug-out shelf and read out the names of those who had been left messages. Then he put the rest back.

The great spire of Chimney Rock was visible forty miles away. "Injuns call it the big tepee," Moss Murphy said, but

Luanna thought it looked more like a giant haystack with a stovepipe sticking out at the top.

"I'd like to take a potshot at that," Tawny Crawford said. "Bet I could knock the top clean off."

"That's the way Tawny is," Belvidry said. "Always knockin' things down. He don't know a lickspit about buildin' up."

When they reached Scott's Bluff the next afternoon, they were only a few days out from Fort Laramie. *The bluff was a blue mountain when I first saw it,* Luanna wrote in her diary.

> *Then it became a great fortress with a castle and turrets on top. I was real surprised when we got up close and saw it was only a pile of yellow rocks. Some say a trapper was once left here, and he starved to death. Others claim he was killed by Indians. I'll be glad when we leave this place.*

The Thomas baby was fussy at suppertime, and Sarah Thomas brought him over for Luanna's mother to have a look. "Poor little mite," Mrs. Hamilton said. "He's got a stomachache for sure. I can brew him some tea, but if he doesn't seem better soon, you ought to have Doc Crane see him."

The tea didn't help. When Doc Crane looked at the baby, he got a worried expression on his face. "Keep him warm," he said to Sarah in a gentle voice. "Give him all the liquid you can get down him." But Luanna saw Doc glance at her mother and shake his head.

"Have faith," Amos Dumfry advised. "Trouble foreseen is overcome." But no one could think of anything encouraging the next morning when the baby was dead.

"He was fine yesterday," Sarah kept saying. She held him tight in her arms and patted his little back. She was singing him a lullaby when they came to put him in a box the men had made from wagon planking. David Thomas took the baby from her, but she kept on singing. While Amos said a few words over the grave, Sarah stood close to her husband, rocking gently back and forth, her arms crossed in front of her and one hand patting gently. Folks never heard a word Amos Dumfry said. All they remembered was the sound of Sarah Thomas's song.

The wagons moved on, but David Thomas came running for Mrs. Hamilton the following night. "Sarah's mighty sick," he said, "and my stomach don't feel right well, either."

Doc Crane was already busy at the other end of the train, for the sickness had struck half a dozen families. "There's a hospital at Fort Laramie," Captain Jeffers kept saying. "We've got to push on."

"Hospital beds don't cure cholera," Doc Crane said, and the dreaded word spread through the camp. Mrs. Hamilton went from wagon to wagon with Doc Crane, wrapping blankets around the sick and giving them tea to replenish lost fluids. By morning, Sarah and David Thomas were dead, and the sickness was spreading.

There was no way to push on now. Those who were well were busy caring for the sick, and the sick couldn't travel. The camp was strangely silent, except for sudden outbursts—fearful-sounding moans and cries. "My wife's gone," Jake Whitcomb groaned. He came to Mrs. Hamilton holding the baby that had been born on the trail. "What am I goin' to do without Elizabeth?"

He handed her the baby and staggered off away from the camp. Some of the men found him a few hours later and brought him back, but he didn't live the night.

Amos Dumfry's wife, Pearl, offered to take the baby. "I can handle two as well as one," she told Luanna's mother.

Luanna hated the sound of shovels scraping sand, for it

was the sign that the sickness had taken another victim—someone who had been fine the day before. When a woman screamed from the far side of the camp and Doc Crane went running, Luanna sat before the fire and covered her ears. I can't stand any more sounds of death and heartbreak, she thought. But Aunt Clara saw her and began to scold.

"No use doin' that," she said. "It won't change a thing."

Doc Crane told Captain Jeffers to order the camp moved. "This spot is tainted," he declared. "We'll all be dead if we don't leave the filth behind us." So they left the wagons of the dead behind them and moved to a spot that was nothing but barren ground.

Then they waited for the sickness to strike again. "I think we've got it licked," Doc Crane was telling Luanna's mother the next evening when Ben came staggering into camp holding his stomach and retching. Mrs. Hamilton sat up with him all night, and Luanna's father paced back and forth, back and forth. Luanna dozed off toward morning and awoke to see Aunt Clara holding herself around the middle crying softly. "Why couldn't it have been me?" she asked. The tears ran down her old face, following the paths of her wrinkles.

"Not Ben!" Luanna cried. She wanted to take Aunt Clara by the shoulders and shake her until she denied it. "Oh, no, Aunt Clara. No!"

"I've lived my life," the old woman mumbled. "I'm almost done. I would have gone in his place."

Luanna was shocked when she saw her mother. Her face looked thin and drawn, and her once dark and shiny hair hung in limp, dusty strands around her face. The sound of hammers soon filled the air—the men had once again taken planks from a deserted wagon to make a coffin. This time, however, there was to be no trailside grave.

"I'll not leave him here alone," Luanna's mother said.

"He'll be buried at Fort Laramie where—where he'll be safe." Her voice trembled, and Luanna knew she was thinking of the wolves that came and dug up the graves and left bits and pieces along the roadside. "I won't leave him," she said again. "Oh, Daniel, I can't."

Luanna ran from the camp, down toward the river where a clump of cottonwoods made a refuge. She put her arms around a tree and laid her cheek against the bark. Ian found her there, holding on as if she would never let go. He took her in his arms and held her tightly, resting his head against her hair.

"Oh, Ian," she sobbed. "He can't be dead!"

He pushed her gently away until he could see her face. "He was alive the whole time he was here," he told her. "I never knew a person so alive as Ben Hamilton."

Ben was buried in the cemetery at Fort Laramie two days later, and Eli carved the marker for his grave. *Benjamin Matthew Hamilton*, it read. *1834-1852. A Gentle Word Is Never Lost.*

Amos Dumfry started to read from his Bible, then handed it to Luanna's father instead. "It's fitting," he told him. When they lowered the box into the ground, Mrs. Hamilton put out her hand.

"Oh . . . my boy," she said. That was all. She put her head on her husband's shoulder, and he led her away.

That afternoon the sky turned black and the rain came, washing the dust away. When the sky cleared, the plains were clean again.

Sixteen

"When folks talk about Fort Laramie, they don't tell you the grasshoppers are thick as fleas," Amy Douglas complained.

Luanna agreed. She had been crunching them under her feet, picking them off her clothes, and trying not to notice when they got in her food. It was even worse at night when the gnats and mosquitoes swarmed. She swatted and scratched until her skin was red and sore.

Fort Laramie was 640 miles from the jumping-off place at Westport Landing, Missouri. It was supposed to be a rest stop where repairs were made, supplies of food laid in, and trailworn clothes mended and washed. All those things are happening, Luanna thought, except for the resting part. As soon as camp was set up outside the walls of the fort, work commenced, and there seemed to be no end to it. Luanna hung the last of that day's washing on a rope stretched between the wagons and went to stir the stew pot. Eli had shot some prairie chickens that morning, and Aunt Clara started right in talking about hot soup.

"It's what your mother needs. It'll go down easy and keep up her strength."

According to Doc Crane, Luanna's mother didn't have much strength left. "She took care of dyin' folks for days, then went and lost one of her own," he told Mr. Hamilton, shaking his head. "Rebecca Hamilton's a strong woman, but everybody finds a limit."

Mr. Hamilton put his arm around Luanna. "We'll give her a rest and she'll be better after a few days. You can take over, can't you, Lu?"

He smiled at his daughter but his face looked pale and thin. Luanna knew how much he was missing Ben—Ben's death had been hard on them all—but it was her mother she was most worried about. Mrs. Hamilton walked often to Ben's grave and stood a long time staring at it. She hardly ever spoke, and she didn't eat except when her husband insisted.

Luanna finished with the stew pot and went with Aunt Clara and Emmie to the trader's store inside the thick adobe walls of the fort. They bought flour, sugar, coffee, and a little bacon. There were Sioux Indians all about, mixing with the trappers and trading at the store. Luanna thought the Sioux were handsome people.

"See how graceful they are," she said to Emmie. Aunt Clara raised both eyebrows and hurried them along, but Luanna kept right on looking. *The men are tall and strong, and the women are slender*, she wrote in her diary that night. *They talk to each other in soft voices, and they look cleaner to me than most folks I'm traveling with.*

Moss Murphy took Emmie up on his horse the next day and rode around the camp with her. "I'm Captain Jinks of the Horse Marines," Moss sang. "I feed my horse on corn and beans." When he brought Emmie back to the wagon, she was singing, too. Mrs. Hamilton picked her up and hugged her hard, but she still went and stood by Ben's grave till suppertime.

By the end of the third day, the oxen had new iron shoes

for the rocky trail ahead, and the wagons were repaired as well as they could be. "There's nothin' more to keep us here," Captain Jeffers announced. "Better turn in early tonight and start off first thing in the morning."

That night while everyone packed there was a ruckus when Doc Crane's traveling money came up missing. "I want to see in your saddle bag," he told Tawny and dragged him over to where the dusty saddle bag lay.

The money was there, every bit of it. At first Tawny denied putting it there, then he blamed it on Belvidry. "She put me up to it," he insisted. "Told me she was tired of bein' without a cent."

When he said that, Eli went for Tawny. Tawny's hand reached for his whip but he didn't have a chance to use it—Captain Jeffers stepped between them.

"I can't abide a liar," he said, "and I reckon a thief's worse. We've got some rough road ahead of us, and we don't need no troublemakers. I'm puttin' you off this wagon train, boy. When we pull out in the mornin', I want to see you standin' yonder, and I want you to stay put till I can't see the fort no more."

Tawny shrugged. "I'll make my own way."

Later that night Luanna woke to the sound of Belvidry's voice coming from outside the tent. She was trying to whisper, but Luanna could hear her just the same. "How could you say a thing like that, Tawny? It made me look as bad as you."

"We're kin, ain't we?"

"That don't make us alike. And it don't make me obligated to let you ride in my wagon all the way to Californy. Captain Jeffers would put us both off this train soon as he found out."

"You're sweet on Eli Hamilton, that's your trouble. Well, he can't drive for you no more. He's got to take Ben's place, so you better let me come along." His voice rose in anger. "Half that wagon's mine, Bel. I'm not lettin' you have it free."

"Take it, then. Take the whole blamed thing, and I hope it falls apart before you've gone ten miles."

Before sunup Belvidry gathered together blankets, clothes, and a few cooking pots and put them in a pile by the Tanner's wagon. Isaac Tanner helped her trade one yoke of oxen for a couple of pack mules. She got Alvin and Sally Sue and made them stand close beside her. "The rest is yours," she told Tawny.

When the train moved out, Tawny was standing by the adobe wall of the fort, same as Captain Jeffers had told him to. Martha Tanner put her arm around Belvidry. "I fixed a spot in our wagon where the young ones can ride when they get tired," she said.

Little Alvin, however, was already tagging along behind Eli, who was preparing to drive the Hamilton wagon. "Come on, then," Eli said, and swung him onto the high seat where Ben used to sit.

Luanna looked back along the line of wagons. She wanted to make a picture in her mind of the fort, a hollow square on high ground above Laramie creek. There were loopholes in the brick walls where rifles could poke out, and a picture of a galloping red horse on the side of the blockhouse, most likely painted by the Sioux. Gray smoke rose from Indian cooking fires and disappeared above the graveyard on the hill where Ben was buried.

A gust of hot, dry wind stung her eyes. When she wiped them, she was surprised to see Belvidry walking beside her with tears in her own.

"I was rememberin' one time when I was little," Belvidry explained after a while. "I got a cut on my foot, and Tawny carried me all the way home along Otter Creek. He washed it and bandaged it up and told me not to cry. Nobody else took care of me like Tawny did." She wiped her eyes again. "Seems like a long time back."

Luanna nodded. She guessed there were all kinds of ways to say good-bye.

Captain Jeffers said ten days would take them to the upper crossing of the North Fork of the Platte. From there, it was only three days to Independence Rock along the Sweetwater River. "That's less than two weeks," Amy said cheerfully. "No time at all."

Luanna thought it was a long two weeks, however. The wagons couldn't always keep to the river, and the trail went up and down hills and across rocky streams as it avoided steep ravines. A few crude signs were posted along the way, warning of disasters that had befallen other travelers: *Bad water. Alkali springs. Poison!* Some of the animals had taken drinks before they could be stopped, and the trailside was littered with gaunt bodies stretched out beside older carcasses that were nothing but bones bleaching white in the sun.

The hot, dry wind made moaning sounds, and the clouds were long ribbons, streaming tattered and torn over the Black Hills. Storms came quickly, flooding the trail and soaking the wagons, but the train rarely stopped except for noonings and nights.

Discarded supplies marked the spots where earlier travelers had been forced to decide what they could live without. Luanna saw a cooking stove and a trunk packed full of winter clothes. A little farther she came upon a rocking chair swaying slowly back and forth, as if somebody had just gotten up and walked away. A butter churn sat atop a rolled-up rug, and a large table was rapidly gathering dust. When they passed boxes filled with books, she wanted to stop and take some.

"Don't be foolish," Aunt Clara told her. "We'll likely be leaving some of our own things before we're through."

How can we put our belongings out by the side of the road? Luanna later wrote. She thought of Ben and put down her pen. How she missed him—his ready smile and gentle humor. Things don't matter, Luanna thought. It's people that count.

She was putting her diary away when she saw something strange in the corner of her memory box. She picked the thing up in her fingers, then dropped it, catching her breath. There is only one person who would kill a snake and put its rattle in here, she thought. She could almost see Tawny's face, laughing, waiting for her to scream with fright. But she hadn't screamed. Instead, she carefully shut the lid of the box. That dried yellow-brown rattle would be a good reminder of the days along the Platte.

When they got ready to cross the North Fork, Amos Dumfry looked at the deep water and said, "Let us pray that there is a source of strength within us."

"You don't need to pray, Amos. There's a ferry that operates all day long," Justin Hubbard told him. But when Mr. Hubbard found out the ferry was run by Mormons he made his wife get inside their wagon and stay there.

"Why'd he do that?" Emmie demanded of her father.

"Because Mormon men can have more than one wife," Mr. Hamilton said, smiling. "I guess he thought one of those men might take a fancy to Eunice."

Emmie put both hands over her mouth. "*I* wouldn't want her," she whispered.

Amos Dumfry took a good look at the ferry. "Those men are not of my faith," he said, "but their raft looks right well built." The ferry did carry the wagons over safely, but the men still had to swim the animals. And then it happened. Three of Mr. Hamilton's oxen gave up and drowned before they were halfway across.

"They were about done before they started," Mr. Hamilton said. "We'll have to lighten our load if we expect to keep pulling two wagons."

Luanna was surprised when her mother didn't object. She'd been awfully quiet the last few days, and she didn't say a word when Eli helped his father unload the big claw-footed table that had been in the dining room back home, and the bedstead that Mrs. Hamilton had loved to polish.

When they took out two barrels of cider brandy, Luanna saw Justin Hubbard pick them up and put them in his wagon. Then, when her father unloaded a couple of extra chamber pots, Mr. Hubbard let those be. "I saw his nose go right up in the air when he saw them," Luanna told Amy Douglas.

"Huh!" Amy exclaimed. "He's short on sense, that's all. I reckon most folks can live without whiskey, but a chamber pot comes in mighty handy."

Luanna thought Aunt Clara had lost her mind when she started scraping up the white powder from the dry alkali flats. "Just as I thought," Aunt Clara declared, tasting a little on the tip of her finger. The next thing Luanna knew, she was using the stuff like saleratus—a kind of baking soda—to make biscuits. They ate them hot and covered them with bacon gravy.

"Even if we are poisoned," Nathaniel said, "it sure tasted good going down."

Independence Rock rose from the north bank of the Sweetwater River like the hump of a gray whale. It got its name because a number of emigrants had managed to get there around the Fourth of July. Amos Dumfry thought it would be fitting to read his copy of the Declaration of Independence, even though the train arrived a month later than the Fourth. The train camped nearby for the night, and old and young began climbing the rock so they could carve their names alongside the other signatures that were already there.

"Think you can make it to the top?" Ian teased Luanna.

It was the first chance she'd had to do something with him for days. Emmie stayed with Aunt Clara and they started out. It was an easy climb, but they took their time, stretching out the minutes until they would have to return to camp. When they reached the top, she sat and watched him carve their names in the granite surface. "For all time," he said.

They stood together, looking out across the plain where the Sweetwater River wandered toward them from the west. "We'll follow that water right into the Rocky Mountains," Ian said. He was silent for a moment. "Captain Jeffers talks about a valley in southern California," he continued. "Not gold country, but good farming land. He makes it sound real nice, Lu."

She felt a prickle of excitement. Up to now, all she'd heard was talk about California or Oregon, and those places had seemed like dreamlands. But Ian was talking about a real for-sure spot. A place where people could settle down and stay.

"Does it have a name?" she asked.

"They call it San Bernardino." He smiled. "Sounds different from the names back home, doesn't it?"

She nodded, repeating it softly on her tongue. "San Bernardino," she whispered. "I kind of like the sound."

That night, a family from the state of Mississippi rode into camp and asked to join up.

"We left home near four years ago," said the man, who introduced himself as Richard Montgomery. "This here's my wife, Alma." Then he counted off his children one by one until he'd named nine of them. "Where's Maggie?" he asked the child closest to him.

"In the barrel, where you put her, Pa."

A bright red head poked out from the tail end of the Montgomery wagon. "Can I come out now?" Maggie asked.

"Sure thing, honey." He turned to Captain Jeffers. "I guess Injuns never saw hair that color before. A bunch of 'em rode off with her, and I had to give two oxen and a good mule to get her back. 'That does it,' said I. 'Until we join up with a regular train, Maggie's not gonna be seen.' Sure do hope you folks can take us on. That child's gettin' mighty tired of hidin' in a barrel all day."

It was the first time Luanna had seen her mother smile since Ben died.

"I declare," Mrs. Hamilton said, and she drank the cup of sage tea that Aunt Clara brought her.

Moss Murphy had shown them how to roast buffalo bones in the fire and poke out the marrow with a stick. "Hunter's butter is mighty healing," he guaranteed. Luanna spread some on a piece of bread and gave it to her mother.

Mrs. Hamilton tasted it and made a face. "It's only one step above that pemmican your pa sets store by." She smiled again. "Why don't we share it with the Hubbards?"

The next morning, there was frost on the ground. "Move out!" shouted Captain Jeffers. A short time later they passed a small trading station with a sign in front that said, "Wave if you can't stop." They waved, because Captain Jeffers wasn't stopping.

The Sweetwater River splashed through a gorge called Devil's Gate, then became a tranquil stream that flowed toward them. It began deep in the great Rockies—called the Shining Mountains because of the way the snowy peaks glistened in the sun. Luanna thought the water tasted brackish, but it was better than anything they'd had since Fort Laramie. The grassy valley around the little river was an easy passage through the rugged peaks and ridges that rose around them. They were climbing steadily, but the grades were gentle ones, and it was good to breathe the mountain air.

They stopped at a place called Ice Slough long enough to dig down under the slushy sod to a solid layer of ice. They chipped out big pieces of the ice with axes and put them in the water barrels to cool the drinking water, warm from the sun. But that night they wondered why they had gone to all the trouble. It was shivery cold after the sun went down, and the water buckets were coated with ice in the morning.

It was the tenth of August when they finally left the Sweetwater. The train began to climb to a place called South Pass at the summit of the trail that led through the Rockies. Luanna held Emmie's hand and told her how they were about to cross the Continental Divide. "The Rockies are the backbone of the country," she said. "We've reached the spot where all the streams run either eastward to the Atlantic or westward to the Pacific." It all seemed strange, however, even to Luanna. The South Pass was a broad, treeless plain, and she would have hardly known she was in the mountains except for the cooler air and the snow on the tall, jagged peaks that rose around her.

They stopped for the night at a place called Pacific Springs, which marked the eastern boundary of Oregon Territory. "We've crossed over for sure," Luanna told Emmie, and she showed her where the fresh water was moving westward in a silver stream. Emmie, however, was more interested in a large tick that had burrowed its head into her skin.

"Get it off! Get it off!" she screamed. Tink removed it by touching a burning twig to its backside, but it wasn't the only tick they had to worry about. They had infested the hides of the animals, and Luanna found several crawling on her skirts. That night, everybody shook out their blankets before they went to sleep, and shook them out again in the morning.

Mr. Hamilton and Tink caught some trout for breakfast. "They're beauties," Mrs. Hamilton said. But when Luanna cleared the breakfast things away, she noticed that her mother's food was untouched. Mrs. Hamilton sat by the fire, sipping a cup of hot coffee and pulling a blanket around her shoulders against the cold mountain air.

"Are you all right?" Luanna asked.

Her mother looked up at her and smiled. "I'll be fine, Lu. I just seem to have a little chill."

That night they stopped at Little Sandy Creek. "The trail splits here," Captain Jeffers said, "and it looks like this wagon train will, too. All you folks headin' for Oregon will follow Moss Murphy in the mornin'. He aims to move across Sublette's Cutoff and be at Fort Hall before two weeks go by. The rest of you will come with me. We'll take Hasting's Cutoff and pick up the California Trail along the Humboldt River."

"Why, that's how the Donner Party got in trouble, goin' that way," Doc Crane protested.

Captain Jeffers nodded. "So they did, but that was back in 'forty-six. Those folks lost time when they had to hack their way through the Wasatch Mountains, and they got caught in bad weather in the Sierras. These are well-traveled trails now. If we move right along, we'll make it to Sutter's Fort by the end of October."

It was a time for saying goodbye. Amos and Pearl Dumfry were going to Oregon and were happy to be on their way, but Justin and Eunice Hubbard seemed divided. He and Eunice climbed in their wagon and pulled down the flap for privacy, but everybody could hear them arguing just the same. "There's gold in California, Eunice. What's the matter with you?"

"I'm plumb tired of your shilly-shallyin', that's what. You talked me into Oregon, and that's where I'm goin'."

Captain Jeffers shook his head. "Folks don't leave their troubles behind 'em when they move west. They haul 'em right on across the Mississippi."

Soon after daybreak, about half of the wagons—including the Hubbards'—followed Moss Murphy. The others struck out on the path that led southwest to Fort

Bridger. Doc Crane was California-bound, and so were the Tanners and Douglases. Red-headed Maggie Montgomery walked happily along with Emmie. "I hope we don't see any Injuns," she said. "It's awful ridin' in that barrel."

Luanna counted fourteen wagons in all at the nooning, but by nightfall there was another. Justin Hubbard came riding in late with a determined look on his face. Eunice was with him, but she wasn't talking.

"Move out!" Captain Jeffers called the next morning, and Luanna saw Mr. Hubbard raise his whip and give it a determined crack. Some folks chuckled at the sight.

People didn't think about the Hubbards for long, however. By nightfall, lots of folks didn't feel too well. "I've got a headache," Amy complained. "And there's a rash on my legs."

Doc Crane was kept busy, going from wagon to wagon. Mrs. Hamilton tried to go with him, but he took one look at her and sent her to bed. "It's the mountain fever," he told Luanna's father. Then he put his hand on Mr. Hamilton's arm. "Don't worry, Daniel. Folks can get mighty sick from this, but it's not like the cholera that took your boy."

A shriek was heard from the Hubbard wagon. "I told you we should have gone to Oregon!" Eunice Hubbard shut her wagon flap and announced she wasn't coming out until the epidemic was over. It didn't do her any good. By morning, she too had the rash.

Mr. Hubbard paced around his wagon. "We should've gone to Oregon," Luanna heard him saying. "I felt it in my bones."

Captain Jeffers was talking to Mr. Hamilton. "There aren't any greenhorns on this train anymore," he was saying. Then he glanced toward the Hubbard wagon and scratched his chin. "Some fools, maybe."

Seventeen

It was a few days before the train could move on. Though mountain fever wasn't as deadly as cholera, it made folks pretty sick and they felt weak for a long time after. "We're lucky nobody died," Doc Crane said, but Captain Jeffers responded by muttering under his breath about losing time.

Luanna, who otherwise felt fine, thought she'd never worked so hard in her life. Her mother and Emmie lay together in one wagon, and Eli lay with Tink in the other. Mr. Hamilton put up the tent for the rest, then crawled in himself. Aunt Clara wouldn't admit she was sick until she almost fell in the fire, and Luanna had to half-carry her to her mother's wagon and tuck her in. Nathaniel, who also felt fine, kept the fire going and did whatever else he could, but it seemed that all Luanna did was fetch and carry, cook and scrub. When she heard that Ian and Amy Douglas both had the fever and their father wasn't feeling too fit either, she fixed a big pot of soup to help tide them over.

"I declare," she said to Belvidry, "I almost wish I was sick so I could go lie down."

Belvidry laughed. "I thought the same thing until I recollected I didn't have a wagon to lie down in."

Luanna thought about that. How would she feel if *she* was all alone, like Belvidry, with two young ones to take care of? She went back to the Hamilton wagons to check on her family, then put on a big pot of beans and fried some bacon. Her folks wouldn't get over the fever if she let them starve to death.

Three days later, when Captain Jeffers finally gave the signal to move out, those who could walk, did. Many, however, didn't feel well enough and were carried in the wagons. A lot of the furniture and equipment that had been moved out to make room for the sick never was put back, and the campsite was littered with things folks were leaving behind.

Luanna's father unpacked her mother's maple dresser to make a little more room. Mrs. Hamilton looked at it a minute, then said, "If I can leave my firstborn by the side of the road, I guess a piece of furniture doesn't matter much."

When they reached the Green River, they were in Utah Territory. By the time the train ferried across, Emmie was well enough to splash her hands through the water. "This river's not green at all," she said. "It's as gray as the fur on a kitten."

Little by little, those who'd been sick got back on their feet and took to the road. Luanna's mother, however, looked thinner and paler than ever, and she tired too quickly. Luanna saw her father watching and knew he was thinking about the long trip ahead. "We've got to look after your mother," he told Luanna. It scared her when he talked like that, with such a solemn look on his face.

Fort Bridger was hardly more than a few log cabins with some Indian tepees scattered about. A trading post and blacksmith shop were inside the stockade, which looked

like a big horse corral. When Captain Jeffers told them the
Snake Indians were friendly, Luanna was glad to hear it,
for there were plenty of them about.

They stopped for two days—long enough for the men to
see about wagon repairs, and the folks who had been sick
to rest up a bit. On the morning of the third day they
started on the Mormon Trail. It took the wagons into the
Wasatch Mountains—high, rugged, and deeply sliced with
brush-filled canyons. Luanna drew in her breath sharply
when she saw how steep the precipices were and how close
the wagon wheels came to the edge of the cliffs. "I can't
look over the side," she told Belvidry. "It makes me dizzy
to think about it."

"I felt the same way," Belvidry told her, "but Eli told me
we ought to think on all them folks that came through
here before us. Eli said there wasn't even a trail back then.
Folks had to cut their way with axes, and they weren't real
sure what was on the other side of the woods." She
stopped to peer over the edge of a cliff. "Might be a bit
scary still, but Eli says it's passable enough."

Luanna walked along beside her. "You think a lot of Eli,
don't you, Bel?"

Belvidry looked straight ahead. "I'm not ashamed of
that."

"No need to be. He thinks a lot of you, too."

That night at the campfire Luanna smiled to herself,
wondering what Nancy would say if she could see them
now. *How I've changed*, she wrote. *I think it must have
started that very first day, when I looked back at our home in
Midford Falls and knew it belonged to Aunt Prue. Change isn't
something that happens all at once. It creeps up on you
unawares.*

It was eight days later and the end of August when the
winding trail led at last down a steep slope into the valley
of the Great Salt Lake. "This was all a wasteland," Cap-

tain Jeffers said, "until the Mormons dammed the streams and irrigated the land. That was back in 'forty-seven." He shook his head as if he couldn't quite believe it. "You'll be able to buy fresh milk and eggs here, but we're only passing through. One good night's sleep, and we'll be off."

Luanna thought the town was an oasis in the desert. Adobe houses sat on wide streets in the town. Farmlands were plowed and planted. She could see the fields of maize and sorghum, and there were fruit trees and vines. Wild sunflowers raised their heads, and crops of hay were being stacked. Captain Jeffers said there was a main street with stores and a real post office. But the distant salt flats glittered in the hot sun. Beyond the town were miles and miles of desert and more mountains to cross.

"It's a long ways from nowhere," Belvidry said, "but these folks did a mighty good job with what they got."

Captain Jeffers led them to a good camping spot near a canyon north of town. There was water from a little creek and firewood in the hills. Other emigrants were already there—folks who had arrived several days before and were resting up and making repairs. "It's late in the season," people were saying. "We're low on supplies, and our oxen can hardly stand." Some had already decided to winter over and start again in the spring.

That night families sat around their fires and talked until late, for there were decisions to be made. "I'm not after gold," Jeremy Douglas declared. "I want a place where I can farm good land and build a home for my family. That little valley Captain Jeffers told us about sounds mighty nice to me. I'm for heading southwest to San Bernardino."

"You've got the Mojave Desert to cross," Justin Hubbard argued. "I heard what happened to those poor folks who tried it a few years back. Part of the trip was so bad they called the place Death Valley."

Isaac Tanner shook his head. "That's because they didn't keep to the main trail. Plenty of folks have made a safe trip, and they didn't have to worry about getting froze to death in the High Sierras, either."

The talk went on. "I said I'd take you to California, and that's what I'm goin' to do," Captain Jeffers told them. "Don't matter to me what part you want to end up in. You can stay right here for all I care, but you'd better make up your minds."

Justin Hubbard was determined to follow the gold trail, but most of the others were ready to find a place to settle down. "I've climbed enough mountains," Martha Tanner said. "I'm looking for a green valley, with plenty of trees and lots of water."

"I don't much care where we go," Amy Douglas confided to Luanna, "so long as we get there pretty quick."

It was finally put to a vote. They decided Captain Jeffers would lead the wagons southwest across the Mojave Desert. Everybody was happy with the decision except Justin Hubbard. He decided to join up with another party that was leaving in the morning and heading across the Sierras. "You've lost your mind," Eunice told him. "What's a schoolteacher like you to do in those gold fields?"

Having decided not to travel through the Sierras, Captain Jeffers wasn't in such a hurry. They wouldn't have to worry about snow and there was time to rest and replenish supplies. "If you can't cross the Mojave in early spring, you'd best wait till fall," he told them. "The middle of summer is hot enough to blister a snake while it crawls."

Luanna's mother tried to get back into her usual routine, but Luanna watched her carefully, bound not to let her overdo. "I can manage," Luanna told her, and her mother gave her a grateful smile. One day Luanna washed some clothes and Aunt Clara cooked up a pot of cornmeal mush. There was butter and fresh milk to put on it, and Mr. Hamilton had bought potatoes to roast in the fire. She was surprised when he came to the wagon for supper carrying a basket of chickens.

"They won't last long on the desert trail," she predicted.

"They won't have to. We're staying here, Lu."

For a second, her mind went blank. How could they be staying when the others were already packing up to go? "We're moving out day after tomorrow," she said. "Captain Jeffers—"

"I've spoken to him already. The way I see it, we don't have any choice. Your mother isn't strong enough. She hasn't been the same since Ben . . . Well, she just won't make it if we don't give her a little time to pull herself together." He put his arm around his daughter. "We're only going to winter here. First thing in the spring, I'll join us up with a wagon train. There'll be plenty of others heading for San Bernardino."

"Your pa's right," Aunt Clara put in. "Your mother is just starting to get her strength back. She's no way fit to travel in a wagon train."

Luanna looked over to where her mother was sitting in Aunt Clara's rocking chair with her eyes closed and her head resting on the chair back, and she remembered the long, hard days along the trail. Her father was right. They didn't have any choice but to be left behind.

I never expected this, Luanna wrote. *Ian is going to California without me. I don't even want to think about that. We're "Winter Mormons" now. That's what the folks in town call us. We don't know a soul. We're here, but we don't belong.*

It was mid-September when the wagons were ready to leave. The night before, Luanna walked with Ian along the creek. He took her hand and held it tight. "It won't be for long," he told her.

"Seems like a long time to me. I heard Captain Jeffers say the trip will take upwards of two months. Even if we take the first wagon out in the spring, we won't reach San Bernardino until sometime in June. That's nine months from now—the better part of a year. Oh, Ian, it *is* a long time!"

He put his hands on her shoulders. "You know I don't want to leave you, Lu."

Then his arms went around her, gathering her close to him. "I want you with me—always. I—I love you, Lu."

"And I love you, Ian Douglas. I've known it for a long time."

She raised her face and felt his lips touch hers. He held her there in his arms a long time. She wanted to remember this moment. She felt so happy and safe, it didn't seem possible that anything could separate them.

But when he walked her back to the camp, she knew that the time had come to say good-bye. "I'll be watching every wagon train that comes into the valley," Ian promised. "If you're not there by the middle of June, I'll come looking for you."

Luanna nodded and tried to smile. But when he took her into his arms one last time, she buried her face in his chest and cried. "I'll be so lonely without you!"

Early the next morning Luanna watched the wagons pull out. Ian took Luanna's hands and held them tight, looking at her for one long moment before he turned away. Amy came up and threw her arms around her. Then she climbed up on the seat next to Ian. "I'm riding for a change," she declared.

Luanna saw Eli and Belvidry standing off to one side talking. Suddenly Eli reached out and took Belvidry in his arms—right in front of everybody.

When he released her, his face was red, and Belvidry looked flustered, but she managed to come over to tell Luanna good-bye.

"I'll miss you, Lu, and all your family," Belvidry told her. "We'll be watchin' for you, come spring."

"Good luck, Bel." Luanna was surprised to find the tears

gathering in her own eyes. But Belvidry was smiling. Impulsively, Luanna reached out and hugged her. "Belvidry Crawford," she told her, "you've got plenty of sass!"

Little Alvin Crawford hung on to Eli's leg until Belvidry finally pulled him loose and handed him over to Isaac Tanner. The wagons began to roll. For a while, there was a long trail of dust to look at, but it finally disappeared. "They're gone," Emmie said. "What'll we do now, Lu?"

There was only one thing to do, Luanna decided, and that was to go on living.

The hot days ended and the weather was lovely, with cool breezes coming down from the canyons. The great mountains that rose in dramatic peaks from the floor of the high desert valley looked so close in the clear air that Luanna felt she could reach out her arm and touch them. The cooler weather seemed like a tonic to her mother. She smiled more often and didn't sit apart by herself so much. One day in October she asked Emmie and Luanna to take a walk with her along the creek. Later, when Luanna fixed a pot of stewed chicken, she ate two helpings.

Mr. Hamilton and the boys managed to fix up an abandoned cabin before the bad weather arrived. The first of November brought an early flurry of snow, and all the folks who were wintering began to wish they had some of the warm clothes they had thrown away back on the prairies. But the snow soon melted, and the soft, warm days of Indian summer arrived. Luanna's mother went outside one morning and sat in the sun. When she came back in, she looked around at the little cabin as if she were seeing it for the first time.

"My land!" she said, and she began searching for the broom. When her husband saw her sweeping, he took her in his arms and swung her around the room until they were both out of breath.

Aunt Clara took her pipe out of her mouth. "Well!" she said, and the corners of her mouth twitched.

Mrs. Hamilton still tired easily, and she had to lie down every afternoon, but she brushed Emmie's long hair and told her stories, and she pulled Nathaniel onto her lap and laughed when he wiggled and said he was too old for that. One day, Tink brought her an armful of dried wild-flower pods on long stems, and she put them in a big crock and set it on a table.

"Just like home," Luanna said.

Her mother looked at her a minute before she put her arms around her and hugged her tightly. "You've made it homey, Lu. You're the one who kept things together while I was sick."

In December, the icy winds came and blew in gales that lifted salty spray from the Great Salt Lake and carried it across the town. "We paid good money for salt at Boon's Lick," Mr. Hamilton said, "and now it's dropping on us from the sky."

As the winter progressed, Luanna and her mother developed a daily routine, and the weeks seemed to melt one into the next. Monday was wash day, and they scrubbed the clothes on a board and boiled them in the big iron kettle. On Tuesday they mended, and Aunt Clara helped, criticizing Luanna's stitches a lot less than she used to. Wednesday and Thursday were set aside for special projects like soap-making. Luanna thought they made enough soap to last through their first year in California. On Friday they always cleaned the little cabin so thoroughly that Luanna felt as if they were turning it inside out. When Saturday came, they baked, and it was good to have plenty of cornmeal and flour again.

Every day, she sat down for lessons with Emmie and Nathaniel, but Tink begged off. "I'm thirteen now," he said. "I've got to help Eli and Pa."

Though her days seemed to pass with a steady rhythm, Luanna was restless. *I'm wearing out my time*, she wrote in her diary one morning, *the same way I wear out the heels of my shoes. I wonder what the folks in California are doing right now. I wonder if Ian ever thinks of me. All I can do is wait. . . .*

Then she put on her coat and took Emmie for a walk in the snow. They saw a black crow swoop low over the trees. "I wish I could fly," Emmie said. Luanna showed her how to lie on her back in the snow and spread her arms in the shape of wings.

"You can't be a bird, but you can be an angel," Luanna told her. Emmie did it again and again until Luanna could no longer resist the fun. The two of them lay on their backs, laughing and flapping their arms, and the hillside was soon covered with impressions of angels.

"I'll never forget this day!" Emmie exclaimed at last. "I'll remember it always."

Luanna got out her diary again that night. *Waiting isn't going to be enough*, she wrote. *I have to live each day. There has to be something worth remembering.*

By the middle of March, the snow began to melt, and the alkaline soil glistened like hoar frost in the sun. When the first blades of green grass appeared, Mr. Hamilton began reading advertisements in the *Deseret News* for wagon trains headed west. "We'll be leaving soon," Luanna's mother promised her. The same day she spied the season's first songbird, her father came in with good news.

"There's some wagons leaving next week," he said. "We'd best start packing."

It was the end of March and there were still patches of snow on the ground when the Hamiltons loaded their wagons for the last time. They planned to travel forty-five miles south of Salt Lake to Provo and join a larger wagon train near Utah Lake. Luanna listened for the wagon-master's cry, and one week later, it finally came. "Move out! Move out!"

She watched the wheels begin to turn, and she felt her spirits lift. "We're almost there," she said to Emmie.

"When I get to California, I'm never, never going to journey again."

Aunt Clara heard her. "Humph!" she said, and she took her pipe out of her mouth and banged it against the side of the wagon. "You young folks are always looking to the end of the journey. The end isn't your goal. It's the trip itself. Haven't you learned that yet?"

It sounded like something Amos Hubbard would have said. But as Luanna walked along behind the wagon, she found herself turning the words over and over in her mind.

Eighteen

From Provo, where they joined the larger wagon train, they traveled southwest along a road that followed an old Indian trail. Small Mormon settlements had been built up along the way, and people were calling this the Mormon Corridor. Melting snow from the nearby mountains filled the creek beds with running water, and there was plenty of grass for the livestock. The days were warm and sweet. Even when folks were eager to reach their destination, it was a temptation to take long noonings and rest in the shade of the cottonwoods and willows that grew along the green banks of the streams.

"We've got the worst behind us," they were telling each other, and no one seemed to be in any big hurry—except for the wagonmaster. He was a man by the name of Jeremiah Kincaid who had been a captain in the Mormon Battalion. Luanna told her mother she thought he acted like he was still in the army, shouting orders and hurrying people about when everyone could see there was no great rush. Her mother, however, said she should wait and see—Jeremiah had traveled this trail before and knew what he was doing.

"It seems pleasant enough now," Mr. Hamilton added. "The weather's good, and folks feel like they've made a fresh start. But when we hit the dry desert, we'll be glad we didn't tarry and let the hot weather overtake us."

Jared Tucker had wintered over in Salt Lake the same as the Hamiltons. "I wish he wasn't coming with us," Mr. Hamilton said. "He's the kind of man who's always pulling sideways."

"It can't be too bad on the desert," Jared Tucker argued one morning. "We survived the Great Plains, didn't we?"

"Some of us did," Mrs. Hamilton told him, and Jared didn't say any more.

The Tucker wagon drew a place in line that day right in front of the Hamiltons' wagons. Mr. Hamilton shook his head. "It's bad enough listening to him. Now I'll have to eat his dust," he muttered.

"Don't pay him no mind," said Aaron Best. "He's full of air and don't know which way to blow."

The Best wagon was right behind the one that Eli drove. "It's a good thing, too," Mr. Best told Aunt Clara. "If you fall off the back of that wagon, you're goin' to want somebody friendly to pick you up and dust you off."

Aunt Clara looked at him sideways, but all she said was, "Oh, pshaw!"

Aaron Best and his wife Susanna were people Luanna liked right from the start. They had come all the way from Independence with the same train that brought Mr. Tucker. "We learned to ignore Jared Tucker before we reached the Platte," Susanna Best said.

One night on the trail, Mrs. Best unwrapped a wad of soft cotton cloth and took out her mouth organ. She ran up and down a few scales, then settled into playing . Then her husband began singing, and their two little boys right along with him. "Oh, Su-si-anna, don't you cry for me. I'm bound for Californy, and my washbowl's on my knee!"

The wagonmaster didn't care how much singing went

on at night as long as everybody got up in time in the morning. He had a bugle that he blew because he didn't like to waste gunpowder. He blew it long and loud, and there was no escaping the message. The wagons rolled early, before the breakfast fires were hardly out. In little more than a week they had come one hundred miles down the Mormon Corridor and merged with the Old Spanish Trail along the Sevier River.

"We could turn left here and go all the way to Santa Fe," Aaron Best teased.

His wife shook her finger under his nose. "I'm bound for Californy," she reminded him.

It was the first of May when they drove through a narrow canyon not far from the southern border of Utah Territory. They found themselves in a place called Mountain Meadows—a gently sloping mountain valley surrounded by high hills—and made camp at the south end, where there was good spring water and lots of grass. "We'll stay a few days," Captain Kincaid announced, and everybody stared at him, scarcely believing the good news. "The livestock can feed," he told them, "and you can rest up for what's coming."

It was hard to believe they would be crossing the desert soon when the land around them was so fresh and green. Luanna took Emmie's hand and walked barefoot in the grass. *It's peaceful here,* she wrote in her diary. *When we leave, there will be nothing but the songs of birds to fill the air.*

At night, in the little valley, folks sat around their fires and visited. They seemed to talk more softly, so as not to disturb the quietness of the place. When Susanna Best took out her mouth organ, she played sweet songs, and the sounds drifted upward and mixed with the rustling of the trees. "It's good to be in a place like this," Luanna's mother said. "Anybody who comes here is bound to be glad."

Captain Kincaid let them stay three days. "It's about the

last place we'll find good grass before we take to the desert," he said.

When they followed the trail again, the days all at once seemed warmer, as though summer had suddenly come upon them. Four days out of Mountain Meadows they crossed over into New Mexico Territory. The landscape gradually changed, and the wind that blew over the land was dry. There was water in the streams, but not enough in the ground to keep the grass green. A week later they came to a great, flat valley that seemed to spread in all directions and was fenced in by far-off mountain ranges with rugged cliffs and rain-washed ridges. Captain Kincaid told them its Spanish name: *Las Vegas*—The Meadows.

"I'm sorry, Captain," Susanna Best told him, "but it doesn't resemble any meadow I've ever seen."

Artesian springs rose to wet the dry, sandy soil, and the oxen quenched their thirst in the pools formed by the water. But it was an arid land all around them.

"It looks so empty," Luanna said, and the wagonmaster heard her.

"Empty?" He threw back his head and laughed. "It's hot and dry, and it's mighty rough travelin'. But the desert is never empty. Open your eyes, girl! You're about to see things you never dreamed of!"

When the wagons rolled in the morning, she thought she had never entered such a bleak and barren land. Mile after mile of sand and rock stretched across the landscape, relieved only by the distant mountains, rising like far-off islands. She helped Emmie tie her bonnet. "Your skin will burn," she warned her.

"It's already burned, and this bonnet makes me sweat. I don't see how it can be so hot when there are clouds in the sky."

The clouds drifted above, thin and white, as wispy as an old woman's hair, but the sun burned relentlessly through, heating the land. At the nooning they rested in the shade of the wagons, then pushed on. "I'll walk with you a while," Susanna Best offered. "My boys like to sit with their pa on the driver's seat, but I get right sick when that wagon sways."

Luanna liked to talk to Mrs. Best. She saw things that other folks passed right by—comical roadrunners that chased after gray lizards, jack rabbits that darted out of sight between rocks, shadows that shifted and changed colors against the mountains. When she heard about Luanna's memory box, she said, "You ought to press some desert flowers, Lu. There are lots of different kinds."

Luanna discovered them growing on rocky slopes, along dry washes, and in tiny crevices. Then the train reached a place called Resting Springs. They stopped to replenish their water supply, and Captain Kincaid told them they were in California. *The spot doesn't look any different from the rest of the desert,* Luanna thought. She spied a desert primrose and gently plucked a yellow bloom. Emmie was looking for flowers too. "Look, Lu, I found a new one!" she cried. "You can put it in your box, and when we see it, we'll remember this place."

The wagonmaster urged them to fill every available container with water from the springs. "We may be in for a dry spell," he warned them.

The next day, about midmorning, Nathaniel set up a yell. "Look! Look!" he shouted. "There's a lake, with lots of trees!"

Everyone was excited except the wagonmaster and the animals. "They know there isn't any water," Captain Kincaid explained. "They can smell it."

It was a mirage, Luanna wrote that night. *It looked so real, the water all shiny, and the trees so tall and thick. But when we drew closer, it got smaller and smaller until it disappeared. What a strange country this is.*

She wrote about a dry lake they crossed, its surface as cracked as a broken platter. Another time she told of a hillside dotted with Joshua trees, their strange, thick shapes silhouetted against the sky, branches raised as if in prayer. Early in the morning she rose to see the false dawn, when lavender light poured over the mountains thick as syrup, and the morning star was like a single lantern in the sky. She walked through bushy plants that looked as soft as lamb's wool, but were brittle and gray, and caught and pulled at her clothes.

When Tink found a desert tortoise, everybody had to take a look at the swirling designs on its dome-shaped shell and the short, thick legs that carried it slowly across the sand. Emmie screamed and said, "Keep it away from me!" But Susanna Best went right up and put her hand on its thick, brown shell.

"You don't have to be afraid of this little critter," she said. "A tortoise never harmed nobody. Look how it's pulled its head inside the shell. Why, the whole thing's no more'n a foot long."

On the second day from Resting Springs a small band of Mojave Indians crossed the trail on their way west across the desert to trade with coastal tribes. They were good travelers, the wagonmaster said. The men could cover one hundred miles in a day. But Luanna was more interested in the way they looked. They wore breechcloths made from soft willow bark, their faces were painted in bright colors, and their hair hung long down their backs. She couldn't help staring at the beads that dangled from their noses and ears. Captain Kincaid said they were friendly enough. Luanna wondered if she looked as strange to them as they did to her.

It was almost June now, and the days were getting hotter and hotter. *Since Resting Springs we have seen no water,* Luanna wrote. *Last night we camped by a dry river bed. Cap-*

tain Kincaid says the water went underground, but that doesn't help us when we're thirsty. It's good that we will reach Salt Springs tomorrow, for our water supply is almost gone. I am dirty all over, and I have never felt so dry.

They reached Salt Springs at sundown the next day and found nothing but a dry hole. "Ration carefully the water you've got left," Captain Kincaid told them. "We'll rest awhile, then move out before sunup."

"My oxen can't go no more," Jared Tucker complained. "I'm not movin' from this spot without water."

The wagonmaster gave him a long look. "Then I reckon you'll stay," he said. He went from wagon to wagon telling folks to unload what they could do without. "It's more'n two days to Bitter Springs. Your oxen will have a better chance if you lighten your load."

Nobody had much water left. They had counted on filling their barrels at Salt Springs. "We'll only drink when we have to," Mr. Hamilton announced, "and then it will be one swallow at a time." He looked at the oxen and shook his head. "Poor critters. I wish I had enough to give them some."

He began to unload their wagons. "I guess we could have traveled easier if we'd left these things home, Rebecca. Prue could have used them."

Mrs. Hamilton only shrugged. "We didn't know, Daniel. How could we have known?"

Aunt Clara saved a few articles of clothing out of her trunk and said they could leave the rest. "If we don't reach water, I'm not going to need my Sunday best," she told them. Luanna noticed how tired Aunt Clara looked. Tired, and old. Her wrinkled skin had a thin, transparent look, and there was a flush across her cheeks. But she was as sassy as ever. "Never mind. I'll make me a brand-new outfit soon as we get to San Bernardino," she declared.

Chairs and tables, tools and clothing, even sacks of flour

lined the trail. Folks who had two wagons were leaving one behind and doubling up their oxen to pull the other. Susanna Best gave Luanna a nudge and motioned toward Jared Tucker's wagon. "Did you ever see the likes of that? Makes about as much sense as savin' food that's gone bad." She shook her head. "If we ever get through this desert, I don't aim to come trailin' back to dig up my leavin's."

Mr. Tucker had scraped out some shallow holes in the sand and buried his belongings, one by one. He was marking the spots with wooden crosses, and when he was finished, it looked like a group of trailside graves.

"Don't he look proud?" Mrs. Best whispered. Then she began to laugh. "Wait until the wind blows. Just wait!"

The wagonmaster came through camp looking at the livestock. "We won't have to worry about the Pah-Ute Injuns sneaking into camp and rustling off our stock," he told Mr. Hamilton. "They'll take about anything that walks, but I think they'd pass these poor critters by."

The men shot long-eared jackrabbits for supper, but no one appeared to have much appetite. The food seemed hard to chew and harder to swallow when there was no water to wash it down. When Emmie touched her dry lips and saw blood on her fingers, she began to cry. "I'm cracking open," she sobbed. Her mother took some of the precious water, bathed her face, and gave her a few drops to drink.

It seemed like the middle of the night when they started out again. The moon was high, and stars were still visible above. Nearby, a coyote called, sending up long, hollow wails. Suddenly, the air was filled with high-pitched, yipping sounds and thin, piercing squeals. "They've caught them a rabbit," Nathaniel exclaimed. "By the time those squeals die away, it'll be digested and gone."

Folks didn't talk much that day. Everyone who was

strong enough walked and the trail was full of footprints that would be covered with sand by evening. Luanna tried not to think about how thirsty she was. Her lips were cracked, and her tongue felt strangely thick. When she did speak, she had to say her words carefully, or her tongue would stick on the roof of her mouth.

"I can't walk any farther," Emmie said. She sat down in the sand and began to cry, but no tears ran down her face.

"You better walk," Nathaniel told her. "If you sit there, a snake will come and get you." Emmie wailed louder, but she got up on her feet.

The camp was quiet that night, though folks weren't sleeping much. Some of the oxen had fallen that day, staggering to their knees and not getting up again. They were unyoked and left by the trail to die. Luanna tried to write in her diary, but couldn't think of the words to say how she felt. Early in the morning, she took a handkerchief and filled it with desert sand. She knotted it tight and put it in her memory box. That would tell the story, she thought, better than any words.

When they were almost ready to leave, Luanna's father began taking more things from the wagon. He and Eli lifted out a trunk full of clothes and placed it beside the trail. "Better go through this to see if there's anything you want to save," he told Luanna's mother. "The trunk stays." Then Mr. Hamilton reached back into the wagon and pulled out a box. "Pa, wait! Those are the books that Miss Wilson gave me," Luanna cried.

She felt her mother's hand on her arm. "I'm sorry, Lu," she said. "We'll get you more books—I promise." But Luanna hardly heard her. Her father was reaching back into the wagon, and he was taking out . . . her memory box!

She ran forward and held out her arms, taking it from him, holding it close to her. "No, Pa. Please!" Her eyes burned with tears that couldn't come. When she spoke again, her voice cracked, and she felt as if she were choking on her own words.

"Nancy gave this to me. My memories are in here. They're—they're all I have left of home." She held the box tighter. "I'll carry them myself, Pa. Please!"

It was Aunt Clara who went and picked up her shawl from the pile of things she had discarded. "This'll make a right good sling," she told Luanna. "You can tie the ends in front and carry your box on your back, Indian fashion."

Luanna looked at her father. "I can do it, Pa. Even if it gets heavy, I won't say a word."

He nodded his head, and her mother and Aunt Clara helped her twist the shawl around the box, then position the bundle low on her back. Luanna tied the ends in front, pulling the knot tight. Then she turned to Aunt Clara and impulsively gave the old lady a hug.

"My stars!" Aunt Clara said.

When they were ready to leave, Luanna stared out and saw the desert waiting, like a bowl of flour about to be stirred. The sky was golden and the wagon train was already baking in the early morning sun.

"Move out!" Captain Kincaid shouted, and the oxen that could still walk strained at their yokes. Slowly, the wagons rolled.

Emmie looked up at Luanna and took her hand. "Will there be any more flowers, Lu?" she asked. "Do you think we'll find any?"

Luanna squeezed her sister's hand and began walking along behind the wagon. "Of course we will, Em," she said. "But I think we'll leave them be. If we pick them all, there won't be any seeds for next year, will there?"

Nineteen

By the nooning, clouds were beginning to gather. Then rain fell in great drops that hit the sand and disappeared. The oxen lifted their heads, opening their mouths wide, and Luanna tore off her bonnet to let the water wet her hair and run in muddy streams down her cheeks. She licked her lips and swallowed, tasting sand and salt. Then she remembered that they were still a day away from Bitter Springs, and she ran to help her mother put out all the empty pans they could gather to catch the rain.

The shower lasted only a few minutes, but it was enough for everyone to have a swallow or two. "I feel as good as if I'd had a bath," Susanna Best declared.

"You don't look it," her husband laughed. "Appears to me you've been playin' in the mud."

Folks laughed a little, and it seemed that they walked for a while with more spirit, but by nightfall most were ready to drop. "I'd give my wagon to see another cloud," Jared Tucker said, and Luanna couldn't help remembering when Mr. Tucker had said the desert wouldn't be too bad.

Captain Kincaid had them all up and moving the next morning when it was still dark. "It's a ways yet to Bitter

Springs," he said. "The sooner we move, the sooner we see water."

"How do you know we won't find just another dry hole?" Jared Tucker demanded. "And what're we gonna do if we *do*?"

The wagonmaster stared at Mr. Tucker until he looked away. "We'll ride on," the captain said, "if we have to go all the way to the Mojave River."

It was midmorning when the oxen suddenly lifted their heads. They pulled harder, their big eyes bulging and their shoulders straining against the yokes. Shortly afterwards, the call came from the lead wagons.

"Water! There's water up ahead!"

People who had hardly been able to walk began to run, and they ran until they reached the waters of Bitter Springs. They fell on their faces and drank until their parched throats were cooled. The men unyoked their oxen and unhitched the horses and mules, letting the animals drink deeply. Some of the oxen went and stood in the water, cooling their sore feet while they drank. "We'll camp here for the night," Captain Kincaid announced.

"Hooray!" said Emmie. Then she crawled into the back of Aunt Clara's wagon and went to sleep.

They reached the Mojave River late the next afternoon and camped among the cottonwoods. "I keep lookin' at that river," Susanna Best said. "Guess I'm afraid it'll go underground and leave us dry." But the clear, cool water trickled over its sandy bed and wound steadily through the brush-filled canyon.

"Keep an eye out for rattlers," Jared Tucker warned. "Don't sit down on a rock till you take a good look first."

But Mr. Tucker must not have listened to his own advice. First thing anybody knew, he came limping into camp holding on to one leg with both hands. "I'm snake-bit!" he yelled. "Somebody help me!"

The wagonmaster took a look and pulled out his knife.

"Good thing it got you through your breeches," he said. He cut the wound and sucked it, then tied it up with a wad of chewed-up tobacco. Mr. Tucker never said a word—he had fainted dead away.

He was sick for a few days, and when the wagons moved out, he said his leg was paining, but everybody could tell there was nothing the matter with his voice. "You should've seen that rattler," he said. "Six feet if it was an inch, and as big around as the top of my leg! When I seen him comin', I could already smell the poison. Let me tell you, you ain't smelled nothin' as fierce as snake venom!"

Captain Kincaid let out a snort. "It smells pretty bad, all right, but that Jared Tucker wouldn't recognize it from a rose."

A few days later, the mountains loomed larger in a long blue line against the sky. Captain Kincaid pointed out the great San Bernardino range on one side and the San Gabriels on the other. "Cajon Pass winds its way between them," he said. "That's the way we're going."

Luanna caught her breath, for the mountains were overpowering. They rose to rugged peaks, then rose again, each crest higher than the one before it. She didn't see how any pass could cut through such country. She thought of the valley beyond, trying to imagine how peaceful and green it would be, but all she could see were those mountains.

The wagons rolled on, climbing steadily every day. At first the dry hills were covered with a short yellow grass, stubby and windblown, like cut wheat. Then a different vegetation began to appear. "Chaparral," Mr. Kincaid called it. Emmie thought it was a miniature forest.

Scrub oak and manzanita, wild lilac and sage—they grew like dwarfed trees and cast enough shade for hundreds of tiny plants to grow beneath. "I wish I was twelve inches tall," Emmie said. "I would walk under the trees and pick the tiny flowers."

"A rabbit would get you if you did," Nathaniel teased.

Emmie looked shocked, and she stayed close by the wagons the rest of the day. "You've got to stop teasing like that," Luanna said to Nathaniel, but he only laughed.

"You don't see her wandering away anymore, do you?"

Captain Kincaid led the train away from the Spanish Trail six miles west to a place where there was a more gradual grade. "A few years back, folks had to take their wagons apart and lower the pieces over the canyon walls," he said. "This is an easier way."

Even so, it was rough going. When they reached the summit, they prepared to drop down into the canyon on the southern side. They had to stop a day while the men cut down pine trees and fastened them to the sides of the wagons. The thick branches would drag behind and act as brakes. Luanna looked out over the steep slopes and deep arroyos and tried not to think how bad the other way must have been.

Everybody got out of the wagons and the men used ropes to hold them back as they lowered them one by one over the ridge and down a trail that was little more than a precipice. Luanna stayed with Emmie as they crawled down the slope, using the bushes for handholds and digging their heels into the dirt. "My land," Aunt Clara exclaimed, "I'm glad I didn't wear my Sunday best."

After reaching the bottom safely, they rested a day, then moved along the narrows of the river until they stopped to camp in a little cove under the shade of some sycamore trees. "We'll roll out early in the morning," the wagon-master told them. "San Bernardino is only a day away." Suddenly he smiled. "Why, you folks ought to be pretty well settled by the Fourth of July. I reckon you'll feel like a celebration!"

Tink threw his hat in the air and hollered, and so did Nathaniel. Some folks sat quietly and closed their eyes, and a few broke down and cried. Luanna could only think that she would be seeing Ian soon. Emmie hopped up and down and squealed with excitement until Nathaniel told her he'd heard there were grizzly bears in these mountains. She went and stood close to Luanna. Mr. and Mrs. Hamilton didn't pay much attention to the commotion—they weren't seeing much beyond each other.

"I've brought you a long way from home," Luanna heard her father say.

"We *are* home, Daniel," her mother answered.

That night, Susanna Best took out her mouth organ for the first time in weeks and began to play, and folks went from one wagon to another, saying their good-byes. "Tomorrow," folks said over and over, the way people do when they've just learned a new word.

After a while, the camp grew quiet, and the only sound came from the wind, stirring the big papery leaves of the sycamore trees.

Luanna wakened early, when the sky was still gray and the foothills around her seemed like ghostly shadows. On the nearby slopes, blossoming yuccas stood like sentinels. She wrapped a blanket around her, slipped on her shoes, and walked quietly away from the wagons. She found a big rock that jutted out of the ground and climbed up on it, facing the eastern sky.

From down a ways in the canyon came the questioning call of an owl. "Whoo—Whoo?" it asked. Luanna listened, but there was no answering cry, and the sound hung on the air, waiting.

Luanna hugged the blanket around her, thinking of other times and places. She let herself remember the Green Mountains of Vermont—the hills of her old home. She let herself think of Nancy and their friendship, and she smiled to herself when she remembered how they had filled their aprons with the buttercups they picked in Long

Meadow. They had slid, shrieking with delight, on winter ice, and they had giggled, heads close together, as they tasted the sweetness of maple sugar on snow. Never, never would she forget those times.

She didn't need her memory box to remind her of the long, crooked trail she had traveled, of friends made and friends lost, of laughter and tears along the way. The box was nice to have, but she didn't need it. Every single thing that had happened, every person she had met had become part of her life, changing her in some way.

That's why today is so important, she thought. I can't do anything about yesterday, and tomorrow is always just out of reach. But today is here and now. It is all I have to work with.

Luanna wondered if she would ever know all the answers. Perhaps not. But she knew one thing for sure. Every morning was a new beginning.

She closed her eyes for a moment and tried to imagine the green valley that was waiting. It wouldn't be full of strangers. She would see old friends again. She smiled to herself when she thought of Ian, and how he had put his arms around her when they'd said good-bye. She felt a shiver of excitement that had nothing to do with the chill of early morning.

When Captain Kincaid's bugle call broke the stillness, folks got up quickly, as if they'd been waiting. Luanna walked slowly back toward the camp, breathing deeply of the clean, cool air. She passed the wagon where Aunt Clara had been sleeping and recognized the odor of lavender toilet water. The flap opened, and Aunt Clara poked her head out. "What do you mean, wandering around all by yourself in the dark?" she whispered.

"It's almost sunrise," Luanna told her. Then she grinned. "You sure do smell fine."

The old lady's face turned pink, but only for a moment.

"I'm dressing for the occasion," she replied. She stared disapprovingly at Luanna's blanket. "I trust you will too," she added.

By the time Luanna had dressed in clean homespun, and brushed her hair until it shone, the breakfast fires were burning and the smell of coffee filled the air. "Hurry up, there," Susanna Best was telling her boys. "We've got important things to do today."

Important things to do, Luanna thought. *Like building a new life in a new land.*

She looked at the eastern mountains where the sky blazed with its promise of dawn. She watched as the sun climbed over the ridgeline and covered the hills with a golden light. Then she went to help her mother with breakfast.

It was morning. It was another day.

WITHDRAWN

NO RENEWALS!

PLEASE RETURN BOOK AND REQUEST AGAIN.